This psychologically sharp, suspenseful drama is a fascinating look at the fragility of marriage and kept me guessing until the very end. A fine mystery indeed.

NEIL HUMPHREYS - AUTHOR OF *BLOODY FOREIGNERS*

An unputdownable story of suspense, secrets and lies. Alison Jean Lester is a wonderful writer and *Glide* is a wonderful novel.

ANNE-MARIE CASEY - SCREENWRITER AND AUTHOR OF *AN ENGLISHWOMAN IN NEW YORK*

Glide is a novel with all the building menace of the best Stephen King told with the style and compassion of Ann Patchett. The book is as revealing as one of Leo's photographs: full of choices, perfectly observed details, and, at the core, a deeply human truth.

CHRIS HUNTINGTON - AUTHOR OF *MIKE TYSON SLEPT HERE*

PRAISE FOR GLIDE

There is a mystery and a mysteriousness to *Glide*. It is a perfect example of Lester's gift for making you feel like she's sharing secrets. She conjures up richness and depth from the simplest of sentences, and takes you far beyond the corners of the setting into the complex heart of human relationships.

NIALL JOHNSON - SCREENWRITER AND DIRECTOR OF *KEEPING MUM*

ALSO BY ALISON JEAN LESTER

Short Stories

Locked Out: Stories Far from Home

Novels

Lillian on Life

Yuki Means Happiness

Memoir

Absolutely Delicious: A Chronicle of Extraordinary Dying

GLIDE

———

ALISON JEAN LESTER

Photography by
ANDREW GURNETT

BENCH

PRESS

For permission requests, write to the publisher via the www.benchpressbooks.com contact page.

ISBN: 978-1-8381124-3-1 (Paperback)

ISBN: 978-1-8381124-4-8 (epub)

Front cover image, interstitial images and book design by Andrew Gurnett.

Published by Bench Press

www.benchpressbooks.com

For Eva Myrth

ONE

I'm standing alone in the kitchen trying to pour chocolate batter into a cake pan without getting any on the counter. I'm also trying to think of a way into a conversation with my wife about children. It's still a few hours before I need to pick her up from the airport, so I can keep chipping away at the problem for a while.

Liv doesn't want children. We've been together since 1986, over five years, and we've almost never fought, but we've fought about that. It's not that I want them so badly. I just want to know why she *doesn't* want them, and she won't tell me.

The sound of feet on the back steps drags me back into the room, and I wonder why there is no knock. I go to the door and open it. The man I see through the glass of the storm door is athletic, very gently balding, with shiny gold curls behind his ears, and he is lighting the candles on a chocolate cake of his own, although his is clearly professionally made. The November day is cold and flat, so the flames don't waver much. He looks up at me and goes back down two steps so I can open the storm door and lean my head out.

"Can I help you?"

"Where is she?" he asks, smiling as if we share a happy secret.

"She who?"

"Liv!"

I look at my watch. "She's flying back from Norway. It's still a while before she lands. Who are you?"

"Morten!" he shouts. Again the impression of some assumed, shared knowledge, some wonderful surprise. I'm supposed to shout, "Morten! Good God, man, come on in!"

"Morten!" he repeats. "Liv's half-brother, Morten! And you must be Leo!"

"Yes," I say. "Well, that's strange . . ."

"Look," he says, "can I just come in and put out these candles?" Puddles of pink and blue wax are forming in the frosting. Of course there's nothing stopping him from putting out his candles right there on the step, but this reminds me to put my own cake in to bake, so I let the stranger into the house.

I straighten up from the cold oven feeling stupid. I forgot to preheat it. It's not worth turning it on now that there's already a great-looking chocolate cake on the table. The man straightens up from blowing out his candles and we turn to face each other. Something about his large frame, his straight nose and his obviously expensive corduroy trousers puts me on alert. I don't recognize his type right away; I can't read anything in him but his charismatic momentum. My own body language, on the other hand – my tendency to lean forward rather than back when preparing a question – tells him everything he needs to know about my fundamental aim to please. The candles on his rich cake smolder.

"Um," I say, and then take the leap. "Why didn't I know Liv had a brother?"

He opens his large hands. "As you can imagine," he says, lifting his impressive shoulders in a gesture intended to convince me of the reasonable, affable heritage he shares with my wife, "I am as interested as you in the answer to that question." He expects me to laugh, but I don't. I smile, though, and I nod. I raise my elbows and plant my palms on the hard edge of the counter behind me. *My* kitchen counter. *My* kitchen. *My* wife. His *sister*?

"May I sit?" he asks, and I wave a hand with what I hope is just the right blend of hospitality and suspicion. He nods his thanks and pulls a chair into position by the kitchen table. He rests his left arm on the table. The other is free to gesticulate. He waves it to announce an abstract concept.

"Brothers and sisters," he begins, "we never say hello, am I right?"

"I'm an only child," I say.

"I see. Yes. Well, brothers and sisters, we spend long moments . . . years . . . in plain view of each other, but out of earshot, until we finally *truly* encounter each other. And then, of course, hello is foolish." His face is calm, confident, settled. I'm still waiting for the ball to land on a roulette wheel of appropriate attitudes. What he's saying sounds like bullshit, but I need to hear more to be sure. His Norwegian accent is obvious, but not heavy. I've always been impressed by Norwegians' command of vocabulary. 'Earshot'. He continues. "And of course we do not expect to say goodbye, not until death anyway, and even then we generally do not have the chance. We die in obscurity, having traveled beyond each other." He looks wistful, and also pleased. He extends his left hand to toy with the wick of a candle, then considers the black residue on his thumb and finger before rubbing his fingers together.

Five seconds of silence, which don't appear to make him uncomfortable. "So . . ." I suggest, leaning forward. I put my hands in my jeans pockets.

"So!" he says, snapping back with renewed vigor. "So, Liv and I met abruptly, therefore we had to say hello. Simply put, it is this. We have the same father, not mother. It was supposed to be a secret, but we found out. We disagreed about our father, we parted in pain. The whole episode – the hello and the goodbye – was an enormous shock to me. To us both. It has been twelve years today. I thought I'd check in."

"Twelve years?"

"Yes."

"So how—"

He distracts me from asking how he knows my name by asking, "When did you say she'd be back?"

"I didn't say." I look at my watch, and it's time for me to find out if the plane is on time. I say, "Let me call the airline."

Morten looks around the room while he waits. He's clearly assessing the kitchen, which means he's assessing me. Us. I turn my back to him when I finally have someone to speak to.

When I hang up I turn back around and tell him, "The plane is about an hour late. I don't have to leave for the airport as soon as I thought." Hands on hips, I stare at the linoleum. I want to be alone. I have a confession, about children, to construct. A secret to reveal to Liv. I need to get it right in my head. Strangely, though, I also want this visitor to go on talking. I want to understand who he is, but that's not all. He's intelligent, quick, entertaining – the sort of philosopher-athlete that isn't as common in the States as it is in Northern Europe and Scandinavia. Guys like him intimidate American men like me. We want them to like us.

Eyebrows up to indicate a general willingness, lips slightly pursed to show concern, he makes it clear that the next move is mine.

"Coffee?" I say.

Our living room, like our kitchen, is any simply furnished room in any eastern Massachusetts town of 20,000 people, except for the wrought-iron chandelier, a huge iron circle crisscrossed with bulb-bearing spokes that we bought in Norway and shipped over. I turn it on, and Morten sits on the couch with his back to the front windows. I take the opposite armchair, thinking about Liv's and my perfect spring wedding. I know this man wasn't there.

"Delicious coffee," Morten says. "Thank you for making it. I love it when people make me coffee."

He's so talkative it's hard to believe he's Norwegian, but then again, Scandinavians have trouble believing Americans are ever as quiet as I am. The ripples of contentment coming off him make me feel guilty that I'm not having as much fun as he is. I try to settle in my chair to look like we're sitting in my living room rather than his. "Liv doesn't talk about her father. Your father," I say.

He just nods.

I fill the space. "She's never met him, so what was there to talk about, right?"

"As far as we know," Morten says, still nodding.

"What?"

He lifts his shoulders and his palms. "Well, it's been twelve years since I have talked to Liv. I don't know whom she has met and whom she hasn't met."

"Fair enough. But I don't think she has met him. She told me she hadn't."

He smiles slightly, rubs his thumbnail along the weave of the cushion next to him.

"I don't think her feelings about him are neutral, though," I continue, trying to draw him out.

"How could they be?"

"Yeah."

I wonder if that's the end of the subject, but then he says, "As far as I could tell she both worshipped him and hated him."

"Both? I can understand the hating, given that he abandoned her and her mother. He didn't offer any support, did he?"

The man shrugs.

"What was she worshipping?"

"She was clinging to all sorts of fantasies about him when we had our falling out. By the last time we saw each other I still hadn't been able to convince her of the truth. She wasn't willing. She was so unwilling she left the country."

"And came to the U.S."

He nods economically. "As you say."

I can feel his eyes on me as I look into my mug. I dare to ask, "And the truth about your father is . . .?"

"Is disappointing, yes, but not so shocking in the big picture. But he was carved in stone for her. Granite. Big and strong. And there I was, as she chose to see things, running at him with a hammer and a chisel."

I blink a few times. "What *were* you doing, actually?"

His light blue eyes flick up to me from the carpet. I expect a look of surprise at the very direct question, but it looks more like glee.

"Let's put it this way," he says. "I was just being myself. I know I look older than Liv, but I'm not. I'm just bigger, and balder. I was born three years after she was, in fact, in a small town on the coast. Our father had married. A small town, a small house, a small garden, two small dogs." As he speaks, he plays with a hangnail on his otherwise perfect big hands. I don't know why he does this. It sounds like he's describing a very nice place, a very nice childhood, but he looks like he's trying to broadcast that he doesn't care.

"Wait," I say, and he looks up. "Liv didn't know her father."

"That's right."

"So why did she know you?"

He smiles. "Good question. Very smart. Excellent. Well, her mother thought she should. She arranged for us to spend time together."

"Without your father."

"Yes."

"Without either of you being told that you were related?"

"That's right. I would just be dropped off. On some weekends."

"Why didn't they tell you?"

"Her mother would have had to acknowledge who Liv's father was then, wouldn't she? Tor would have had to be available to Liv, and that's not what her mother wanted."

"Her father's name is Tor," I say, pronouncing it the way he had: Toor, with a breathy tap of the tongue against the hard palate on the r. "Your father's name is Tor."

"Yes. Like the god. The noisy one."

"Was Liv ever dropped off at your house?"

"Never."

"And she never saw who dropped you off?"

"That was always my mother. We knew each other's mother. That's what we knew about each other."

I nod, imagining two blond women, two blond children. The story is hardly believable. I feel that I shouldn't believe it. I keep asking questions.

"Did you and Liv always get along?"

He laughs. "No. No, no. Our personalities are so different, and I was younger and naughty. A younger half-brother is as irritating as a younger whole brother, I'm sure, even if you just think he's a friend. We behaved like siblings. But then we wanted to spend time with our friends from school instead. I resisted visiting her, or maybe she refused to have me, probably both, and our relationship ended."

"Until?"

"Until I discovered we had the same father, and went to find her."

"How did that happen?"

"It was easy to look Karin up in Bergen. I went to the house."

"No, I mean, how did you learn you were related?"

His shining face clouds over. "My father told me. He was angry. I don't remember what I'd done to deserve it that time. It didn't take much. So he told me he preferred his other child because she gave him no trouble."

"What a dick," I say, and he smiles appreciatively. "So, you found her."

"I found her. And we caught up, and it was all nice, but then I told her we were related."

I wait for more, but he doesn't say anything. Neither do I, this time.

"What?" he asks, finally.

"What you're telling me doesn't sound so awful. Why would she keep it a secret?"

"I also want to know. I'm very hurt that she didn't tell you about me. But we did part on bad terms."

"So bad that she wanted to erase her brother?"

He arches his back, inhaling noisily through his nose. Once he has exhaled he looks at me. "I opened up to her about him. I told her what it had been like to grow up with him. I thought I could, you know? I thought she would feel like we had both suffered. It seemed to me that she would see it hadn't been so bad to be abandoned by him if it had been so difficult to live with him. But I was wrong."

"She got angry?"

"It was so strange. Angry, yes. She refused to see me again."

"Why wouldn't she tell me this, though? Where's the shame?"

"Well, after that he went to jail, didn't he?"

"He did?"

"Yes."

"What for?"

"Embezzlement."

"So?"

"And was killed there."

"Oh. Wow. But still . . ."

"You really can't imagine wanting to keep him a secret?"

"I really can't."

"Well, I can. She's spent her whole young life creating a wonderful father in her mind. A father full of wonders. She looks in the mirror and wonders if he's the reason she's prettier than her mother. Every time Karin pisses her off she wonders if maybe her father wasn't wrong to get out of there. Then suddenly she has the reality of him shoved in her face. So she rejects the messenger. No, what is the expression?"

"Shoots the messenger."

He snaps his fingers. "Yes! Shoots the messenger. I stop existing. She blocks it all out and returns to imagining her father. It's a nicer picture. It's easier."

"She could have told me this."

Morten shrugs: *Women! What to do?*

I'm not used to trying to unravel mysteries, and I don't like the effort it takes. I need a break. "More coffee?" I ask.

"Yes, please," he answers. He drains his mug and hands it over with a neat sucking of his lips. "I love it when people make me coffee."

In the kitchen I put down the mugs. They are simple and heavy; a tribute, like most of our things, to Liv's sensible, humorous taste. I slide a finger along the edge of Morten's cake plate, picking up stray icing, and eat it. It is rich and delicious, so I do it again, taking a moment to collect myself. I consider throwing out my unbaked batter, but I'd hate to waste it, so I turn the oven on.

Morten chuckles. How long has he been in the doorway? How long has he been in the country, for that matter? I pour him some coffee and cross the kitchen to hand it to him before going back to stand by the oven.

"What was Liv doing in Norway?" he asks.

"What she does every year. Visiting her mother and grandmother in Bergen. Looking for new artists, checking out the shops in Oslo, ordering new stock."

He settles himself at the kitchen table again. I can't help saying, "You're looking quite at home, Morten."

"I feel it!" he responds, hitting my curveball right back at me. "I haven't been with family in such a long time, and there's really nothing like it." He blows on his coffee. "But you were saying, about what she was doing?"

"Yeah. She goes to a pewter fair, looking for new designers. New suppliers. Keeps up to date with the older ones."

"So she's a distributor?"

"She's one of the very few selling Norwegian pewter on the east coast. And she's the best."

I enjoy Morten's broad smile as he appears to share my pride.

"And what do you do?" he continues.

"I teach photography, at Bridgewater State College," I say, "and I exhibit my work in marginal galleries." I quickly follow with, "And you?" before he can ask me another question. "What have you been doing that has kept you away from family for so long?"

"Coaching soccer teams."

"In the States?"

"Unfortunately."

"Hey."

"No offense intended. But it's so serious in Scandinavia. Here the teams seem to come and go with each season."

"But there must be *some* very talented players here."

"Yes, absolutely. Very frustrated people."

"So you've been moving around, I guess."

Morten starts laughing about places he has lived, the singing garbage men in Virginia, the reek of garlic from the next apartment in New Jersey. The oven beeps that it's the right temperature and I put my cake in, and then I go ahead and sit down with him. He regales me for the whole thirty minutes it takes to bake, and at times I laugh out loud. It has been so quiet in the house without Liv.

Then I remember to look at my watch. "I've got to go!" I tell him.

"Okay!" he says, matching my tone, getting up out of his chair at the same time as I do, smiling like me, and it's completely freaky. I don't know what he's doing. I don't know what he's going to do, and it's awkward to ask. It feels like he'll follow me to the door, and to my car as well.

"So, don't you have to get back?" I venture.

"Back where?"

"Where do you live?"

"Atlanta."

"*Atlanta?* You *flew* here?"

"I took a chance. Karin said you were a nice guy."

"When? You talked to Liv's mother?"

"Once."

"Why?"

"To get this address."

"Jesus."

"She said she understood the need for reconciliation."

"So, maybe she told Liv you were coming."

"Maybe. I didn't make her promise not to, although I told her I hoped it would be a surprise."

"Where are you staying?"

"I don't know yet. I'll work something out."

I don't want him with me when I meet Liv at the airport, but I can't leave him in my house. I could ask him to go find a hotel and come back the next day. That's what I have just about decided to do when he speaks.

"How about I come with you so we can find out as quickly as possible why you've never heard of me?"

I don't like it. I hate confrontation, though. For someone like me, a request as reasonable as "Please find a hotel and come back in the morning" to an overbearing stranger feels like a confrontation. So I say "Okay" and we get our coats on.

Morten steps back into the kitchen to move our coffee mugs from the table into the sink before we go out the door.

We get into my second-hand Accord and the doors clack shut and I feel the cold vinyl of the seat through my jeans and the icy plastic of the steering wheel against my skin. Getting into the car in winter, I always feel like I'm synthetic too. I need the heater on full blast for a long time to feel human again. Liv and I are both like this. When we get in a cold car together we don't talk until the temperature is right and our jaws have unlocked. Not Morten. Morten seems physically comfortable right away. He's got his hands between his thighs, but it makes him look more like a happy child than a cold man, and he glances around with curiosity at our neighborhood as we drive out of it. I wonder how he sees it. No one is out on the sidewalk. Even on warm days you don't see many people out. I didn't think about what the personality of the neighborhood might be when we bought the house, just that it was the right house for us, and we could afford it because the neighborhood wasn't fashionable – it was too near the nail factory – and that was fine. The house had grass all the way around it, and a front porch, both of which felt like heaven to me after living exclusively in college housing and dingy apartments. It also had a finished basement, perfect for a darkroom.

We haven't made any real friends in the neighborhood, not just because we haven't made much of an effort but because no one has. Our first winter in the house was a punishing one, and when the tide of snow finally began to go out, receding from the sidewalks and thinning to patches on the lawns, we took long walks around and around the neighborhood and barely encountered a soul. I remember passing one older guy, hat pulled down low over his ears, bare hands in his jean-jacket pockets. I was preparing to greet him when he came into comfortable hello-saying distance, but he spoke before I could. Just one word. "Spaass." Then he disappeared behind us.

After five or six steps, Liv said, "Spaass?"

"He meant 'sparse'."

"Oh! Why did he say that?"

"I think he was commenting on the snow."

We laughed so hard we had to hold onto each other.

I'd like to tell Morten this story, to bring Liv into the car with us, but I'm still too cold to talk. I think about asking him where he got his coat, as it must be warmer than mine. I think about asking him if he's been to Massachusetts before. I think of asking him what Liv was like as a child. In the end he asks the first question.

"Did you grow up here?"

"Closer to Boston," I tell him.

"Nice?" he asks.

"Okay," I say. "Quiet."

"Too quiet?"

Again I feel him matching me, this time reducing the length of his questions to the length of my answers.

"I don't usually think that," I say, deliberately stretching my answer out, and turning the noisy fan down now that the car is warming up. "Sometimes I wonder what I'd be like if I'd lived somewhere more lively."

"Nurture rather than nature?"

"Maybe."

"Well," he sniffs, sitting up to his full height, "it was quiet where I grew up too, and I'm loud."

I can't help but smile.

Until we're actually at the passenger exit from international arrivals and I'm imagining Liv coming through the doors, I'm glad Morten is along.

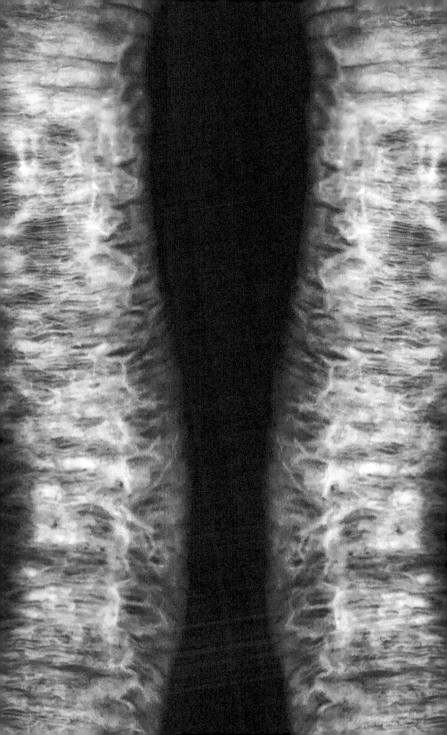

TWO

Liv's plane lands, but she doesn't come out with the first groups of passengers. The periods between groups grows longer and longer, and eventually enough other planes land to bump Liv's flight off the arrivals monitor. We have to wait at the Scandinavian Airlines counter until the staff for the evening departures arrive. Of course we call the airline from a pay phone while we wait, but they don't have the passenger manifests. I'm not sure the SAS staff in Boston will either. We might need to call Oslo, or the headquarters in Stockholm, but it's already after midnight there. Finally, a man and two women walk along behind the counter to their places, putting down their bags and arranging things the way they like them, before one of the women looks up at us and indicates with a wide, red-lipsticked smile that her bit of the counter is open for business. Her badge says her name is Maria Teresa, and I worry irrationally that she won't be able to help much because her name isn't Eva, or Astrid, but I tell her our story.

She can't help us. She's not allowed. Nobody is, actually.

She's sorry. "Was she visiting someone there?" she asks help-fully. "You could call them."

"I'm calling Karin!" I tell Morten as I take off for the bank of pay phones again, pulling out my wallet as I run. I have my back to him as I read out my credit card number to the operator, but I know he's right behind me. I can feel the heat off his body. I hear the distinctive *bleat-bleat* of the ring-tone in Bergen and I imagine it waking Karin up, but I know she won't mind. The anticipation of relief has me twisted up tight. I'll find out where Liv is. I'll find out who Morten is. But the bleat doesn't end and Karin doesn't believe in answering-machines.

I hang up. Morten finally steps back out of my space when I begin to turn around.

"Now both of them have disappeared," I say.

Morten's shoulders move in what looks like a quiet laugh.

"Why aren't you worried?" I demand.

He looks at his watch, calculating. "One a.m. isn't late for an adult to be out. And she's a performer."

I nod.

"Also, is Karin still single?"

"Yes."

"So. Many reasons to be out."

"Okay. We'll try again later. Wait. Maybe Liv's on the next flight."

"Is there one?"

Before I can answer, Morten turns and jogs back to Maria Teresa. I walk toward the counter and see Maria Teresa shake her head. All the SAS flights for the rest of the evening are departures.

Morten comes back to me, shaking his head too. "Any-way," he continues, "wouldn't she have called to say so?"

"She would have." A chill shudders up my body. Not on my skin. It's deep in my spine.

"Let's go home," I say. "I can call Liv's hotel in Oslo if we go home."

The hotel number is on a pad on the kitchen counter. I don't even take my coat off before making the call. Liv usually stays with a good friend when she's in the city, but this time Barbro is away visiting her own mother. There's an arts and crafts fair on at one of the central hotels, Hotel Bonde-heimen, so she decided to stay there. Every time I called her in Oslo, she sounded fine. She sounded great. The craft fair was wonderful. Fairs always make her want to stay in Norway, as she hasn't yet found a community of artists in New England that gives her the same feeling of wonder as Norwegian artists do. She was particularly taken with one jeweler, but that jeweler was a woman, so I didn't get jealous. Liv didn't sound like she was on the verge of leaving me, which is of course what I worried about all the way home.

I ask the woman who answers if Liv is still a guest at the hotel, and she tells me that she is. She connects me with Liv's room, where the phone rings and rings and each ring takes more air out of my lungs. The woman comes back on the line and asks me if I want to leave a message.

"Actually, can you tell me how long she will be staying?"

"Yes, sir. Let me see. Yes. She has extended for one night."

"Just one night?"

"Yes, sir."

"So she'll be on the same flight tomorrow?"

"I don't know that, sir."

I ask her to leave a message for Liv to call me, please. Please make sure she calls me.

I usually like the sound of the receiver going back into the cradle. The type of plastic our phone is made out of is good solid plastic. You can keep it forever, and you want to. Today, I hate the sound. It's the sound of absence. Absence of Liv. Absence of understanding.

"She kept her family name when you married?" Morten asks.

"What?"

"Liv didn't take your name?"

"How do you know that?"

"You said her name. It hasn't changed."

Of course. It's so hard to keep up with him. I experience a sudden wash of fatigue. I take off my coat and pass him to get to the coat hooks. Morten hangs his coat up next to mine, and we return to the kitchen. I can't believe we're about to talk about family names, but I guess it's best to get it over with.

"She didn't take my name, no. She figured her Norwegian name would be more credible for her business."

"What is your family name?"

"Coffin."

His eyes pop wide. "No!"

"Yes."

"Wow." His eyes slide over to the right.

"You've just thought up a bunch of jokes, right?"

"I have! Good jokes!"

I hold up my hand. "I've heard them."

"What about —"

"It's a common name in New England," I tell him, and then I tell him Liv has extended her stay by one night.

"Yes, I heard that," he says, and looks at the floor. I see his thoughts twitch in the skin above his eyebrows. I find I don't want to hear them. I want to know what has happened, but I don't really want to discuss it with him. I'd like to call our best friend, Noriko, but she wouldn't be able to help me in any substantive way. I've just got to find my way through the next 24 hours. I gather my energy together and say, "What shall we have for dinner?" I'm not looking forward to dinner. I just want to feel like I'm in control.

Some minutes later I'm stirring a boiling pot of spaghetti. It doesn't need stirring, but it's something to do. Morten pours a jar of sauce into a saucepan and puts it on the stove, so he's standing right next to me. He turns on the burner. I watch him stir the sauce, tap a wooden spoon neatly on the side of the pan and put it down on a spoon rest I was barely aware of and never use myself. He finds a fork and reaches in front of me to lift a strand of spaghetti out of the boiling water, checks it for tenderness by splitting it with his thumbnail, and nods, satisfied that dinner is coming along nicely. I don't trust this guy, but he's basically making me dinner. I feel sick.

"Shall I go out and get some wine?" he asks.

"No need, I've got some." I retrieve a bottle from a cabinet and put it on the table next to the cakes, bringing a knife to its neck.

"Bowls?"

"Top right cabinet." He reaches up, and then I say, "Wait," and he freezes. "Didn't you and Liv realize you had the same last name?"

Morten unfreezes and opens the cabinet.

"We don't. She has Karin's last name."

"I know that. But Karin's last name isn't Tor's last name?"

"They never married." He puts the bowls by the stove and reaches in front of me again to pick up the pot and pour the spaghetti into a colander I put in the sink.

"Really?"

"Why would I lie?"

Why didn't I know that Karin and Tor never married? When Liv told me that her father left when she was a baby, I assumed there had been a divorce. I never asked about it because she wouldn't have remembered it.

"There aren't as many stigmas in Scandinavia as there are in America," says Morten, obliquely answering my unspoken question. He sees right inside my head. While we eat, I finally ask what Liv was like as a child, and he says everything I want to hear.

Morten is very efficient with the dishes. By the time I've made a pot of decaf and am pouring a cup to take to the base-ment, hoping that doing some developing will calm me down, help me pass the time, he's drying his hands on the dish towel, hanging it up neatly, and moving through to the living room. He turns on a light by the couch, walks over to the bookshelves and stands with his hands in his pockets. I see him lean over to look at the titles on a lower shelf and then remove a hand from a pocket to turn a photo to face him. Liv. A black-and-white but sunny photo, taken before we were married. I call it "The Shepherdess". It's all smile, cheek-bones, and short pale braids. He looks at the photo a long time, but doesn't say anything.

Down in the basement, bathed in the hellish red light of my darkroom, I hang dripping photos, scrutinizing the images as I dry my hands. The dripping slows. I stop at one.

Liv. An expression of loving surprise on her face. Soft smile. Cheekbones. Short hair. My eyes roam her face. Black-and-white photos of people with light blue eyes are even more arresting than color. Hers are alien eyes. They're not really even blue, like the ocean isn't, and the sky. The filaments of her irises are white. When I concentrate on them, I feel as if they're not even eyes. They're distractions. Somewhere underneath the impossibly pale irises there must be normal ones – brown ones, or muddy green ones like mine – doing the normal things eyes do. Being married to Liv for five years hasn't accustomed me to the way she looks.

Morten and I are making up the bed in the guest room. I can't believe he answered the phone without calling me up from the basement to talk to the hotel myself. I feel small, and resentful, and I really don't want him sleeping down the hall from me, but the living room couch is too short and inhospitable. I still can't bring myself to be rude. Oddly, we have the same bed-making standards: tight hospital corners, sheet and blanket tucked in at the end but not at the sides. Interrupting the rhythm of the exercise, I say, "It doesn't make sense that she would have the hotel call here for her. She could have told us about taking tomorrow's flight herself."

"I know," he says, and I wait for him to add something else but he's pulling the heavy bedspread up onto the end of the bed for me to take one side of.

"Why wouldn't she want to make the call?"

We pull the bedspread up over the pillows.

"I don't know. We'll ask her," he says and straightens up, hands on hips, assessing our work.

"And it's such a strange time. It was what, three in the morning or something in Norway when she called, right?"

"That's right."

"Was she right there when they called?"

"I don't know."

"Did you ask them where she was?"

"I didn't think to, no."

"Let's call them back."

"Okay," he says, and lets me get to the door before saying, "I think we can probably assume she was there when they called."

I stop in the hallway. "Are you sure?"

"No, but it would make sense. She was out when you called, and they would have given her the message when she got back, right? Then she would have asked them to call you."

After a moment I say, "This isn't the sort of sense I'm used to."

Morten laughs at this. "What a great way of putting it," he says. Even at such a moment I find myself pleased that he likes how I talk.

Then I say, "Or she told them to call and went up to her room before they did. Or they slid a message under her door and she called down to reception to ask them to call."

"You're making her sound like such a coward."

This gets my back up, but I don't respond. "Come on," I say instead, "I'll show you the bathroom."

I'm proud of the guest bathroom. The long pale walls show my large framed photos off well. Liv has warmed the space with a woven rug.

Morten puts his toiletries bag on the back of the toilet and feels around inside for something. I stand by him, waiting to hand him a towel. He says he can't find his toothpaste.

I open the mirrored door of the medicine cabinet. "There's some extra in here." I take my hand off the cabinet door to reach for the tube, and he holds the door open himself so I won't close it right away, looking calmly at everything inside.

Suddenly I'm exhausted again. I hand Morten the toothpaste and leave him staring into the cabinet. I retreat to my bedroom and close the door behind me.

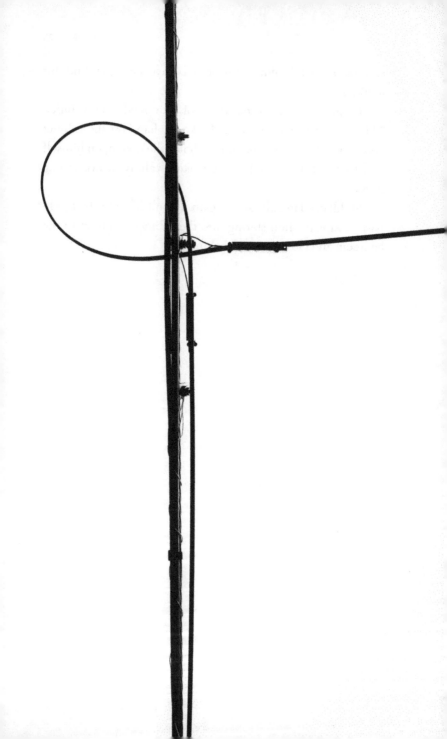

THREE

The kitchen clock says 6:24 a.m. I'm brewing coffee. Despite yesterday's confusion, I've slept well. I think I was relieved enough by the call from the hotel that I blocked everything else out. I didn't have it in me to spend any more time wondering about Morten, and I didn't call Karin again. I just fell into oblivion. When I woke up and remembered everything, I felt concern, sure, but number one in my mind was Liv's return. It still is as I look out the window and breathe in the coffee smell and wait for sunrise with a tingle under my skin.

I hear Mozart from the living room. Morten enters the kitchen quietly, wearing the same outfit as the day before. I'm happy to see him because now I can share my relief and my excitement with someone. I decide to talk amiably. "Liv is crazy about Mozart."

"I see," he says amiably back, and opens the fridge, looking around in it. Then he says, "Just a moment," and moves in long strides out the back door to his rented car, a little midnight-blue BMW. He returns, flushed, with a bottle of champagne. "Mimosas?"

I'm not used to people who change their mood so quickly, but I get caught up in his energy's slipstream, and soon I'm pulling orange juice, butter, and raspberry jam out of the fridge. Morten reaches in under my arm for some cheese. "You have a cheese slicer?" he asks.

"Is there a Norwegian without one?" I answer.

The toast pops up.

We arrange food on our plates, mix our drinks and clink our glasses. "To Liv," I say.

"To life," he says.

"Same thing," I say, and he smiles.

We eat standing, looking out the window.

"Today we rake the leaves?" he says. "For the homecoming?"

We cut diagonally across the driveway to the garage, talking about my mother, who died of lung cancer when I was in college. I had asked him about his, and he replied, "She was beautiful. Like yours, right?" I let his hook grab me by the mouth and drag me uncomplaining into reminiscence.

"Beautiful?" I say, and think about it as I rummage through a box for two pairs of gardening gloves. "She had a nose like Bob Dylan, and brown stains between her teeth. Let's just say she wasn't the subject of quite as many of my portraits as Liv."

Morten laughs, a loud "Ha ha!"

I can only find one pair of gloves and Morten tells me he doesn't need any. I pull our two rakes from the wall, taking the old one and giving Morten the new, and we head over to the side yard. "Your mother was very young when she had you?" I ask. I'm looking at him but he has started raking.

"Uh-huh," he answers, and then really gets to work, accompanying himself with a song in Norwegian. The way he sings it makes it sound dirty.

It's wetter than yesterday, and heavy. The leaves aren't very lively, but there are plenty of them. They stick to our shoes and their dampness seeps up our trousers. On days like this I'm more aware of the gasses puffing out of the nail factory. They hang around.

Morten shouts to me across the yard, "Have you played much soccer?"

"A bit," I shout back. "It was the only sport I had any respect for at boarding school."

"Boarding school, eh?"

"Yeah, well, my mother was worried I'd get lost in the shuffle at the local high school."

Morten laughs. "And would you have?"

"Absolutely."

"You have a ball?"

"Not really."

"No, I mean, do you own a soccer ball?"

"Oh! Ha. Sorry. Yes. Somewhere." I head back into the garage. Morten puts down his rake and starts stretching his calves. We undo all our raking, faking each other out with my old gray ball.

My father died of a heart attack when I was two and my mother didn't spend time with other men after that; at least, not when I was home. Other than at boarding school, where the range was pretty limited, I wasn't exposed to many different male types. I never had a sibling. I had friends, but I don't remember boisterous play. We were

more of the Snakes and Ladders, Scrabble, and eventually
Yahtzee types. Yahtzee made us feel particularly high spir-
ited. I don't remember a *really* competitive opponent,
though. At boarding school I studied, did photographic
essays, and went home to my mother for truly sympathetic
companionship. She always made me potato pancakes with
lots of sour cream, "to build up your strength," she said, as
if what I was doing at school was somehow heroic. She
took me out sometimes, to hear music, or to see a play –
once she offered to take me to a baseball game; I declined –
but I could always tell when she wanted to be reading
again. She was a book reviewer. I learned to refer to her as
a literary critic, but I never observed her being critical. I
just saw her reviewing books: looking at them, again and
again.

People were accustomed to me being on the fringe,
observing, documenting everything, and that was fine. They
expected to see me there, and missed me if I wasn't, but
didn't necessarily want to talk to me. The boys, I mean. Girls
sometimes liked to talk to me. I took nice photos of them, and
I listened, only because I didn't know what to say when they
talked, but they didn't need to know that. I know for a fact
that I was one of the few boys at boarding school who had sex
as a junior rather than a senior, and I was certainly the only
Yahtzee-playing boy who had sex at all. It was just the once,
with April Quinn, who presented me with her body as a sort
of thank you, I think. A gift. I'd done really nice graduation
photos for her.

As we wind down and survey the destruction of the leaf
piles we've raked, I'm thinking that I can't remember ever
having so much fun with another man.

"Need some water?" I ask him.

"Only if you do," he says with mock machismo. "What's for lunch?"

"Oh, cake. Or . . . cake."

"Fantastic," he says, and claps a hand on my back. He makes me feel young, almost like a little brother, as we go in together.

"Do you have to work tomorrow morning?" he asks once we've taken off our coats and shoes.

"Nope. I'm done with classes until after Thanksgiving."

"Oh! Right! Thursday, right? Well, I'll be out of your hair by then." He's looking down at his damp socks. Suddenly, Thursday seems too soon.

"No, no, Morten. Stay, if you can. We've never actually had family for Thanksgiving."

After a pause he says, "Shouldn't you ask Liv if it's all right with her?"

"Yes. I should."

He smiles. I look at the floor.

"I'll ask her when she gets back and tells me who the hell you are."

"Okey doke."

"Where the hell'd you learn to say that?"

He launches into a story, and I open the fridge and pull out a carton of milk to wash the cake down with.

Later I show him the darkroom, and he looks only briefly at the now-dry photos hanging in there. "Nice, nice," he says, nodding, appearing to ignore the ones of Liv, and asks to see the camera I took them with. We go back up to the kitchen where the light is better and I show him how to use my Nikon FE2. His hands look too big for the delicate dials, but he's able to manipulate them very precisely, and starts to take my photo. Being photographed gives me an uncomfortable chill, like I want a heavier sweater. "Relax," he says. "You're worth looking at too, you know." I put my hand to my forehead to move hair out of my eyes that has never in my life been in my eyes.

He asks to see more of Bridgewater, so I drive him around the college. On the way home it's obvious to him that I'm struggling to formulate a difficult sentence. "What is it?" he asks.

"I kind of want to go to the airport alone this time," I tell him, just about succeeding in an effort not to sound over-apologetic.

"Of course you do," he says.

"You're sure?"

"I'll have dinner ready when you get back."

At the airport, I'm surprised to see Noriko standing near the arrivals gate. She's checking out the beautifully manicured nails at the ends of her plump and tapering fingers. "Magenta suits you," I say from right behind her, and she shouts in surprise.

"Woah! Wait, wasn't Liv expected yesterday?"

"Tell me what you're doing here first."

"Picking up my parents," she says, with both eyes back on the doors. "They went to Japan to see the leaves change color and get drunk with the uncles, remember? But what about Liv? I didn't call so you could have some time alone."

"That's nice of you. But she didn't show."

"Why not?"

"I still don't know."

"Why not?"

"I don't know that either."

"But you know she's coming now?"

"I'm hoping. I know she only extended her hotel stay for one more night."

Noriko nods. "Fingers crossed, then."

"There's something extremely weird going on."

"Sounds like it."

"Yesterday her brother pulled up out of nowhere in a fancy car, bearing a cake, pouring champagne—"

"Liv doesn't have a brother."

"She does now. A half-brother."

"Really?"

"Well, I think so."

"God. What's going on?"

"I don't know."

"Oh, yeah, I forgot. What's he like?"

"He's . . . Well, he's really fun, actually."

The doors swing open for one, two, three, five, eleven people, and I stop counting and start calculating. Roughly three hundred people on the plane, maybe two-fifty. Even if half of them transfer to other flights, that's still over a hundred to count. Liv could be last. Someone has to be. Noriko and I talk about how awful it is to be one of the last people standing at the luggage carousel while the crowd thins and everyone else is released into the next part of the journey.

"Sometimes it's hard to shake the sadness when your bags finally come out," Noriko says.

"And the bags come out looking a little sheepish, don't they?"

"I always think they want to say, 'Well, imagine how *I* feel!'"

This makes me smile, and I imagine Liv watching fewer

and fewer bags pass her on the carousel. I hope that's what is happening. I hope the worst that will happen today will be the disappearance of Liv's luggage.

"Speaking of which," says Noriko.

"Of what?" I ask, eyes never leaving the doors.

"Of feelings. How do you feel?"

"Alarmed."

"I bet," she says. "I can't imagine what it's like to have a stranger in the house."

"Oh, him," I say.

"That's not alarming?"

"He's okay," I tell her, "and when Liv gets here he won't be a stranger anymore. But where is Liv?"

It's now mostly Asians emerging through the doors.

I greet Noriko's parents with her. "Call me if you need me," Noriko says into my ear when we hug. "I'm not working tomorrow."

After I've waved them off I go to the toilet, praying I'll see Liv looking for me when I get back, but she isn't among the confused hoverers. I have her paged and wait by the information desk.

I drive home.

I can't reach Karin despite the late hour.

"Two nights in a row with a toy boy, maybe?" Morten suggests.

I ignore this. "The only thing I can imagine is that she's performing."

"Both are possibilities. But it's so late. Would she still be out if she were performing? My money's on a gigolo." He's trying to make me smile, but I won't.

"She could be at a music festival," I say. "She does that a lot. If I knew which one I could call the local hotels."

Morten says, "Try her again as early as you can tomorrow morning. If she's not at a festival she'll be at home. Singers don't get up early, right?"

"Good idea." I reach for the phone again. "Now I'll call Liv's hotel."

"Why not let me?"

"Their English is perfectly fine."

"It might go more smoothly though, don't you think?"

My internal reaction is to think not. There was nothing wrong with how the conversation went last time. But then I doubt myself. It's possible we would have had more information yesterday if Morten had been the one to call.

"Maybe so," I say and hand him the receiver, turning the piece of paper with the hotel number on it toward him.

Other than hello and Liv's name and thank you, I don't understand what Morten says at all. I can't even discern where each word begins or ends unless he stops speaking. Not understanding the language makes me feel blind.

When Morten finally hangs up he says, "She checked out this morning."

"This morning?"

"Yes."

"At check-out time, you mean? It's usually eleven, right?"

"He said it was quite early."

"Did Liv say why she was leaving early?"

"He wasn't there when she left, he was just reading to me from the computer."

"Could he ask the person who checked her out?"

"That's what I told him to do."

"So, he'll call us?"

"He'll have to ask that person when they get there, when the shift changes."

"And then he'll call us."

Morten gives me what might be a sympathetic look. Maybe it's actually pity. "It's not his job to call us, Leo. It's his job to deliver the message with our questions. We'll have to call when we get up."

All these words are perfectly clear. I understand all the words now. But I'm still blind.

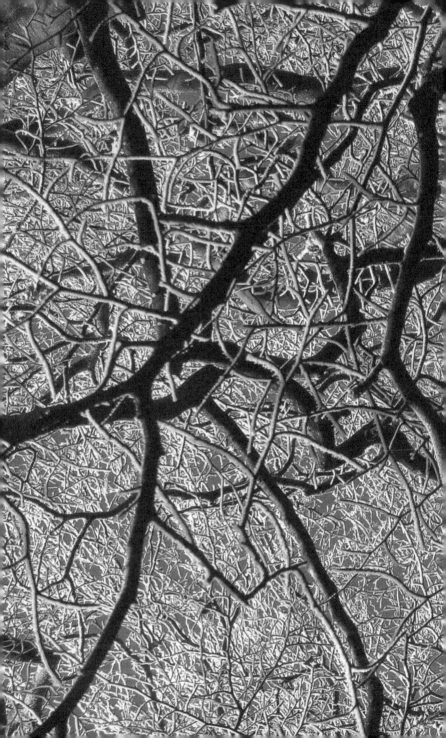

FOUR

I don't know if my 4:30 am alarm is audible in the guest room. I hope not. We have Karin's number on speed dial so I don't have to go searching for it downstairs. It's number one. She's the most important person in Liv's life after me, despite the frequent tension between them, and right now she's the most important person in my life, the key to my sanity.

The phone rings on and on and on and on. I'm afraid to hang up in case Karin is just taking forever to wake up. I'd hate to cut the line right before she answers. She *must* be at a festival. But which one? Liv would know. Damn. And damn: the hotel phone number is in the kitchen. I lie back on my pillow for a while to see if I can remember it. I've dialed it so frequently. I'm sure of the country and city codes of course, and the next two numbers. The final three are also easy to remember. I draw a blank on the middle four. Damn.

My robe doesn't do much to warm me as I tiptoe to the stairs and down. The house is cold, but so is my spirit, frozen in fear – fear of what has happened to Liv, but also of waking Morten. Or just, maybe, fear of Morten. I ask myself what the hell I'm doing sneaking around my own house. So what if Morten hears me? I have every right to go downstairs and call Oslo. But I really want to make this call alone. I even try to dial quietly until I realize I will have to speak in my normal voice, not a whisper, and I have to trust that I'm far enough away from the guest room not to be heard. My feet freeze as the call rings through to the hotel reception desk.

"Hi there," I say when a woman answers. "I left a message yesterday asking if I could speak to whoever checked my wife out. Her name is Liv Svendsen and she checked out in the morning, from room 408."

"Yes, hello Mr. Svendsen. Your message is here, yes. I was here when she checked out."

"You checked her out?"

"That is what I mean, yes."

"You remember her?"

"Yes."

"Did she say where she was going? It was so early."

"I assumed to the airport."

"You assumed, or she said?"

"I think . . . I think I assumed."

"I'm sorry if this feels like an attack. It's just that she was supposed to arrive home in the U.S. last night, and she didn't."

"Oh! Let me think some more. Maybe some shopping? No, she took her luggage. Maybe she went to a friend? When was her flight?"

"It was at seven p.m."

"So maybe she went to a friend for the day and then . . ."

"And then?"

"And then . . . I don't know. I'm sorry."

I can't face tiptoeing back upstairs again so I lie on the

couch under the blanket we keep on the arm in the cold seasons. My feet refuse to warm up. I wonder if Liv was somewhere with Karin? If so, what could be their reason for not telling me? Why would they abscond together? Or were they actually in Bergen, but not answering the phone? Nothing in any of my conversations with Liv had hinted at any change of heart, let alone of plan. She had been excited to be home for her birthday. I'd told her that having her back would feel like it was my birthday, too.

Whatever had happened, was happening, was bad. It was around midday in Norway, so the day would be rolling. Liv would have woken up somewhere, gone somewhere, eaten something. Where? What?

What if she *had* gone to the airport but had taken a morning flight, not back to the States but somewhere else? This thought sets my heart racing. It's a crazy thought, but the dark destroys all rational fences and my fears canter away in every direction. I try to think of someone I know who hasn't been surprised when their spouse has left them. Can't do it. They've all been side-swiped, up-ended, left blinking in the dark like me, silently shouting "What did I do wrong?"

I wake up to the opening and closing of cupboards, the smell of coffee. The sun isn't up yet and the light in the living room is coming from the kitchen. I experience again the strange blend of suspicion and comfort that comes from having Morten around.

He's dressed. He's impeccable. I'm yawning. He's smiling. I sit at the table and pull my feet up onto the rung of the chair to keep them off the cold floor. He pours coffee for us both and hands me a mug. I tip my head to it and breathe in the steam, smiling to show him I'm grateful. I'm confused by a surge of sadness, a prickle in my throat.

Morten says, "Time to call Karin, then?" Too loud. My God he's hearty.

"I already have," I tell him, speaking into my mug. Come on, Leo. Sit up. Straighten your back. Look at the man.

"Oh? When?"

I sit up and look at him. Nothing to be ashamed of. "About four-thirty."

"And?"

"She wasn't there."

Morten folds his arms and turns his head to think.

"Or she wasn't answering," I add.

He looks back at me for more.

"Could that be the case?" I ask him.

"Why would it be?"

I can't help bending back down to the mug in my hands, taking a sip for strength, staying there. I shake my head, no idea.

"So let's call the hotel." He's lifting the receiver.

"I did. They didn't know where she went, but assumed she was going to the airport."

He replaces the receiver and nods slowly.

"Maybe I should go to Norway," I say.

"But what if you cross in the air?"

It's my turn to nod. Then I ask, "So we call the police and report a missing person?"

He looks at his watch. "Not yet. It hasn't been forty-eight hours since she was last seen yet."

"God."

"I know, I know."

I look up at him and he's drinking his coffee. His eyes

look, what? Gleeful? I try to think what I'd do right now if he weren't here. I'd want to talk to Noriko, but it's too early. Other than that, I'm blank.

"So what do we do?" I ask Morten.

"Well, we have to eat, of course, and then, we exercise."

"I can't play games today, Morten."

"Not games," he says, opening the fridge and taking out the milk. "I think we should hike."

"But we'll be away from the phone."

He gets bowls out, his ownership of the kitchen complete. "That's a concern, yes. But you have an answering machine. Change the message. Make it a message for Liv, and we'll go out and walk somewhere. We'll walk fast, burn up the adrenaline."

"I don't think so," I say, standing up and going to the cabinet to choose which cereal I want.

"Okay," he says. "Fair enough. We eat. Then we see."

After breakfast, I spend time in the bathroom, and take as long as I can in the shower, but still the phone remains silent. Morten remains tranquil in a chair in the living room, reading a magazine, but I can't read, and morning TV is garbage.

"Coffee?" I say, after pacing the kitchen.

"Coffee is the last thing we need," he replies.

We walk.

I drive us to the top of Sprague's Hill, which I think is Bridgewater's only hill.

"We couldn't have parked at the bottom and walked up?" Morten asks as we get out of the car. He arches his back to take in the whole of the water tower.

"Nowhere to park," I say, coming up beside him. "But check out these woods."

He turns and we face the trees opposite.

"We can head down that side, and come back up the hill that way," I suggest, and start across the tarmac. Morten follows, asking if there's a trail.

"I don't think so," I say and plunge in, shooting through the fallen leaves as if I know where I'm going. I don't, beyond the fact that no matter how we roam, all we need to do to reorientate ourselves is find where the ground rises again and follow it up. I like the feeling of leading, but then Morten speaks, "Wow," and I turn and realize he has stopped walking. "This is beautiful," he says.

Is it? There are neither trees in full fall colors nor snow. The dominant hue is grey.

"Is it?" I ask.

"Trees, Leo!" Morten says, stepping over a fallen trunk to get to where I am. "I feel so much better when I'm in trees, don't you?"

We start walking again, now side by side.

"Usually, yes."

"But not today."

"Not today."

He claps me on the shoulder. "Try and enjoy it if you can. You might as well. Breathe in the rich smell of all that delicious *decomposition*."

I do as he says and register the interplay of dead leaves, dead wood, and earth. Also taking his lead I pick up my pace and we begin to walk in earnest, lengthening our strides, swinging our arms, until we are suddenly running, not competitively but as one, or maybe it is competitive but only to see who is better at staying with the other one. Side by side we follow each other's smallest suggestions for which ways to move among the trees. The ground flattens out and we settle into a jog, breathing in more and more of the scents we're kicking up, until we come upon the edge of a development – houses with silent above-ground pools, houses with swings and jungle gyms, houses clearly with kids – and we turn as one and sprint away, weaving between the trees along the base of the hill. I'm not thinking anymore. You can't when you're watching your footing and watching the way ahead and sending and receiving signals with your companion. You just behave. You just . . . enjoy.

And then Morten trips, spectacularly, flailing his arms, hitting the ground and rolling onto his back, hooting with laughter. It's excellent. I laugh too, and offer him my hand, but rather than take it he pats the leaves next to him, laughing and panting and sighing. I hesitate, but then instead of lying down I retreat a half dozen steps, start to run and then pretend to trip, imitating his gyrations as best I can. We lie in the leaves under the skeletal canopy and laugh life into the air around us.

Calming down, Morten turns on his side and looks at me so fondly that I fear he might be about to embrace me but then his arm snaps out and he taps my ribs. You're it!" he shouts and jackknifes to his feet before turning and haring up the hill. I scramble up and run after him, but I'm not really chasing him. I don't care if he makes it to the car first. I don't care if he's doing a victory dance when I get there. That kind of thing has never mattered to me, and it won't suddenly become important now. What I do care about is that I am learning to play. I am playing.

· · ·

When we get back to the house the light on the answering machine is flashing and I run to the phone in my coat and boots. I get a cramp in my gut waiting for the message to play.

It's Noriko.

Before Morten can say anything I pick up the receiver but not to call Noriko back. I speed-dial Karin's number, and listen to the bleat.

After I hang up, Morten says, "Coffee?"

I take a deep breath. "I'd actually like tea, but we're out."

I don't feel comfortable in the house. Being outside was much better, and it's still a good while before we can call the police. I say, "We could walk to the convenience store."

Morten puts his coat back on and out we go.

Walking along the sidewalk isn't as uplifting as running in the woods, and soon my mind is churning again. After a block I throw out a question.

"So . . . was your father's death in the news?"

"Yes."

"Oh. Huh. Karin always said she had lost track of what had happened to him."

"And you're surprised? Please. Norwegians are very proud."

"What has pride got to do with covering up for a man who abandoned you?"

A split-second change of gear around the eyes, and then the Scandinavian shrug. "I believe she was ashamed of having known him in the first place."

"How about Liv? Why didn't she ever talk about it?"

"Ashamed of having trusted him?"

I stop. He does too. "Then why did she never mention *you*, Morten? Was she ashamed of you?"

"I would love to know the answer to that. You know I would. I told you the first day I was here."

I check his eyes for trickery. I can't identify any, and we resume walking.

"I'm just a soccer coach," he says.

Right now, I'm inclined to believe him. He looks like a soccer coach. I decide to let that be the end of the questions for the day. I point out the house that always has its Christmas decorations up first.

Christmas music is playing inside the store. Morten gets himself a basket and glides humming down the short aisles, picking up bags of red and green wrapped chocolates, almonds, napkins printed with bells and holly. He tosses them in the basket with a flourish, to the great amusement of an elderly gay couple and the fine-boned Pakistani cashier who works through every holiday. I grab a few bags of popcorn for stringing and dump them into his basket with a flourish, exactly in time with the music.

The carols accompany us outside because Morten is still singing. What the hell, I take a whack at harmonizing. Farther down the road, Morten says, "You know what my number one favorite song is?"

"No."

"'Home on the Range'."

"No!"

"Oh, yes," he says. "Why isn't it a Christmas song?"

"That's such a stupid question."

"Just think about it, Leo. It has all the optimism of any carol, without any of the obligations." He belts out the part of the song everyone knows and then says, "You see. It is just as joyful and triumphant, with no need to be faithful and come and adore. Plus, it's got animals."

"Some people love coming and adoring."

"I'll take antelope and cloudless skies over an all-knowing father-figure any day."

I think about this for a while.

"I would have loved a father-figure," I admit.

He huffs a laugh. "Fathers are overrated."

"You think?"

"I know."

"Don't they teach us things?"

"What did you learn from your father?"

"Nothing."

"You see?"

"He died when I was little."

"Oh, *faen*. So you think he would have taught you things?"

"Yeah."

"Okay. Okay. Maybe he would have."

I look over at him as we scuff through a drift of leaves, and his expression makes me smile. "You don't believe that do you?"

"Nope."

I laugh. "Thanks for saying it anyway."

"Sure."

A few steps later he says, "You want kids?"

"I *have* kids."

It's out before I can stop myself. My face heats up, but he says "Oh yeah?" as if I've said something perfectly normal.

I try to sound normal. "Yeah. Twin boys."

"Where are they?"

Another flash of heat in my face. "Maybe New Hampshire? Someone had a post card from a town called Auburn. But I don't know where they are now."

"Why not?"

"Their mother doesn't want me to."

"That stinks," he says.

"I thought you said fathers are overrated."

"Stinks for you, I mean. Not for them."

"You don't think they want me?"

"Sure they do. We all want what we don't have. Boys with sisters want brothers, girls with brothers want sisters. But it's all a complete gamble."

"Do you wish Liv had been a boy?"

"I never did before, but I do now."

"Why?"

"If she were a boy, she wouldn't be married to you, and you wouldn't be so suspicious."

"Ah."

"Ah."

"Sorry about that."

"It's understandable."

We walk in silence past a couple of houses and then he says, "Anyway, now I have a brother-in-law," and he puts a hand on my shoulder and squeezes it. I feel myself blush a little. He takes his hand away and speaks my thoughts. "We both do."

Another flashing light greets us on our return. I'm so sure it's more likely to be an impatient Noriko than Liv that this time I go ahead and take off my coat and boots. I almost call Noriko without listening to the message, but it annoys me when people do that, so I press Play.

A woman clears her throat, and I know it's Liv. When she speaks her voice is tiny.

"One more day," she says. "My flight gets in tomorrow evening. I, um . . . I hope you're okay."

Then she's gone, and I shout her name at the machine, hands outstretched, as if she might hear me, as if I could catch her. I groan and look around, feeling like I should run outside in case she's still in sight. Her voice was so vulnerable, so intimate. The ghost of her hangs in the air.

"God damn it, Morten! Now what?"

"Do you have a way to reveal the last call that came in?"

I slap my leg. "I do!"

Once it is revealed I jot it down. "She's still in Oslo," I say. Morten has no doubt recognized the city code as well.

"No need to keep trying to reach Karin, then," he says.

I pick up the receiver and dial. The phone rings on the other end, and rings, and rings. Is Liv gone from the place, or is she listening to it ring? I will her to reach out, but eventually I have to give up. I take the receiver away from my ear to the sound of a distant voice. I slam it back against my head. A man is saying "Hallo? Hallo?"

"Hello!" I crow. "May I speak to Liv Svendsen please?"

The man, clearly an old man, speaks in a wavering voice, and I can't understand him. Hurriedly I pass the receiver to Morten.

They talk for an eternity, it seems. When Morten hangs up, all he says is, "It was a payphone."

"God! Why? What is she now, a spy?"

Morten smiles at this, shrugs.

"What else did he say?"

"Not much."

"He talked a long time, though!"

I think he was a lonely man. He told me about why he was in that neighborhood."

"Did you ask about the people around him?"

"It was to buy fish. Yes, I did. I asked him if he could see any petite blond women around him."

"And?"

"He said," Morten says, and then imitates the old man's voice, "Petite, maybe. But blond? They all have hats on.'"

"You could have asked him to shout her name!"

Morten laughs and reaches into a cabinet for a glass.

"What's funny?"

"You can't ask an old Norwegian to shout in the street."

"Even in an emergency?"

"And even if you could, do you think only one woman would answer to that name?"

He fills his glass with water.

"Did you ask him what neighborhood he was in?"

"I did."

While he drinks I say, "We can call the hotels in that area. Maybe Liv changed hotels. Maybe she wanted to save money."

Morten swallows, and puts down his glass, shaking his head. "There aren't any."

"You know the area well?"

"I do."

"No hotels at all?"

"None."

"Not even a tiny one? Those aren't always obvious."

"Do you want your tea now?" he asks, infuriatingly, pointing to the bag of things from the convenience store that I don't even remember setting on the counter.

I rub my temples. "Yeah. Okay. Why not?"

Morten fills the kettle. I get some mugs out so I don't feel like I'm the guest. "Maybe there *is* a hotel there," I insist.

"Maybe there is," he allows, and pulls the tea out of the bag, but I take the box from him and struggle with the plastic wrapping.

"Leo," he says, but I keep struggling. "Leo," he repeats, and I struggle till the box jumps out of my hands and I drop my stupid useless arms down by my sides. I know I must look pitiful but I don't care. "She'll be home tomorrow," Morten says.

We take our tea to the living room and sit down.

"I've been thinking," Morten says, "and I've come up with a good way to pass the time tomorrow."

When did he do this thinking? Has there been time for thinking?

"What's your idea?" I say.

"We look for your boys."

"*What?*"

"Why not?"

"Because, seriously, my heart couldn't take it. Waiting for Liv to come back is enough excitement, thanks."

"I didn't say go and see them. I said look for them. Take the first steps. Get the ball rolling. You really haven't done anything at all during these years?"

"No," I say sullenly and sip my tea. "Wait. I did do one thing."

"What?"

"I asked the college librarian how to find out if someone lived in a particular town."

"Via the phonebook, I would think."

"Sure," I say, "but I'll need *archived* phone books."

Morten's eyes question me over his mug.

"If she has moved away from Auburn," I explain, "I'll be able to tell when. If it's recently enough, I can ask at the local post office if they still have the forwarding order."

"Why don't we just go straight to the post office and ask?" His brain functions at lightning speed, but I have to think for a while to haul up my thought process from so long ago. It's embarrassing, but I persevere.

"Because, I'll have to be able to tell the post office where she *was* living. For that I need the phone books. And, of course, if she's still in Auburn, the phone book will give us her number."

"Okay. So where are the archived phone books kept?"

"Some libraries keep them, the guy said. Manchester would be the closest big one."

Morten puts his mug down with a clunk and gets up, clapping his hands. "Come on!" he says, and heads to the kitchen. When I get there he's already talking to directory assistance, asking for the number for the public library in Manchester, New Hampshire.

FIVE

I can't argue that there's no need to find something to do for another day. I can't argue that I don't want to know where the boys are. When Morten tells me the Manchester library has extensive historical archives including phone directories, I feel a tingle of excitement. I should stay by the phone, though. Rather than decide what to do, I tell him I need to call Noriko, and I go upstairs to the bedroom to do it, hoping it's close enough to lunchtime for her to be free for a few minutes.

"Wait, I just saw her," says the woman who answers in oncology. "Kath," she says to someone near her, "can you do me a favor and run after Nori?" Kath must say yes because the woman asks me to hold. I tolerate a minute or two of muzak before Noriko says hello.

"It's Leo."

"Thank God! I hoped it was. Update please!"

"She'll be back tomorrow evening."

"Oh phew! What has she been doing?"

"I still don't know."

"You didn't ask?"

"I couldn't. She left a message when Morten and I walked to the convenience store."

"Shit. That stinks. How did she sound?"

"She sounded sooooo small."

"Did you call her back?"

I tell her about Liv not being at the hotel anymore, and about the old man answering the pay phone, and about how I felt like I'd just missed *seeing* Liv, like I'd reached a platform just as her train pulled out. My voice must sound desperate because Noriko hushes me.

"Easy, Leo. Take it easy, honey. She'll be back tomorrow."

"How can I be sure?"

It's a second before Noriko responds. "Fair point."

"I'm, um, well, Morten and I are thinking about driving up to New Hampshire for the day tomorrow, to pass the time."

"Good idea."

"You don't think I should stay by the phone?"

"I'm sure I'd want to as well, but I'm also sure it would be a terrible day."

"I feel like I'm being unfaithful or something even considering it?"

"Why, are you attracted to this Morten guy?"

"No, no." Jesus, I'm blushing. "Although it is really weird to be hanging out with him, when the fact that Liv didn't tell me about him can't mean good news."

"I get you. But would you rather be alone?"

"Nope."

"And do you *really* think she's going to call? It sounds like doing it even once was hard for her."

"I just don't want her calling and not knowing where I am."

"So, change the message on your answering machine."

"I did."

"So you're covered. Now can I eat my lunch, please?"

I do that thing when you put two fingers on a map's legend to see how long ten miles is and then hop your fingers along the route you'll be taking. In this way, I guess it will be about a two-hour drive to the library in the morning.

They open at ten so we leave at eight. We drive along flat, three-lane expressways toward a flat, gray-white sky. Trees line the roads almost without interruption, but few are evergreen, and we can glimpse the lives they hide – homes gathered around cul de sacs, a mall, another mall, another mall, a cemetery, a pond here, a reservoir there. I try to deflect another effort by Morten to get me to agree to try and meet the boys if we find an address for Marilyn. He came at me with that once the previous afternoon and again during dinner. "We'll see," didn't work then. Neither did "They'll probably be at school." Those responses don't work on his doggedness any better today than they did yesterday and eventually I overcome my fear of confrontation.

"Look," I interject, loud enough to cut him off properly. "I want to meet them on my own."

"I'd wait in the car," he says.

"Nope. No witnesses."

"I could wait at the library."

"No, Morten. No waiting. No pressure. No expectations."

"But if you —"

"Back off!"

"That's the spirit!" Morten says, laughing.

That's annoying. I was proud of myself for establishing my ground and holding it. But now that he has laughed – and he's still chuckling – it's more like he feels he's the one with reason to be pleased with his effort. Like he's been trying to get me to push back at him all along and has finally succeeded.

Inside the library we're directed from the central rotunda to the New Hampshire Room to do our research. We locate and divide the eight telephone directories covering Manchester and its adjacent towns from 1984 to 1991 and sit down opposite each other at a long table.

"Her family name is Greer," I tell Morten quietly, heaving open 1984, but he's looking around in clear fascination at the people dotted at the other tables. He hasn't heard me.

"Morten," I say, as loud as I dare.

"Sorry," he replies, glancing my way before opening a directory. "It's just that this is a bit like going to the zoo. So many different animals on view. What's her surname?"

"Greer."

There are a couple of Greers in 1984, but no Marilyn or even M. Greer. Okay, I think. Maybe she has family in town. Maybe she stayed with family until the kids were born and she had recovered, then got her own place. I open 1985. Bingo. I turn the book to show Morten, showing him M. Greer sitting between J. Greer and Scott Greer. I could go right back out and call the number, but Morten is working backwards and he shows me that the listing is gone in this year's book. He opens 1990 and she's not there, while I look in 1986. Still there. Still there in 1987, but not in 1989. In 1988, she's gone.

"She left in 1988," he whispers. "Or late 1987."

"Damn." The disappointment is made worse by the thought that she might not have left but might rather have married and changed her name. That would complicate matters, assuming I could find her. And how *would* I find her, in that case? I could call the other Greers and see if they are in fact family. Maybe they could let me know where she is, and if her name has changed. If she married, would the boys have new last names too? If her spouse adopted them, I guess they would. I could look the boys up in the local schools if I knew their names. I hate that I don't know their names, first or last. I'd assumed Greer, but maybe not. I feel bleak, heavy, and just sit for a few minutes, barely thinking.

"So we call the other Greers," Morten says heartily.

I don't want to. It would be very uncomfortable. When I think this I give myself a mental slap. I'll make the calls if I have to, I decide, but first I'll try the Auburn post office. I know it's a long shot, asking if they have a forwarding order on record after several years. But Auburn looks tiny on the map. Maybe they don't get very many and forget to clear them out of the files. I find the post office in the 1991 phone book and write the address and phone number under the 1987 address for M. Greer in a little notebook.

Returning the phone books to their shelf, I tell Morten we'll need to see if we can use the phone at reception to call the post office for directions. "Leave it with me," he says.

As we approach the desk he whispers, "Don't say a word." Then he proceeds to address the receptionist, a gray-ponytailed woman in a gray sweater. He accentuates his

Norwegian accent, and her eyes immediately twinkle. He tells her we are both Norwegian and that we need to call the Auburn post office for directions. Could we possibly trouble her to use her telephone? Of course we can, she tells him, and lifts it from the desk onto the counter for him. He says something to me in Norwegian, making a writing motion with his hand. I take out my little notebook and pen again. When someone answers the phone at the post office he smiles at the receptionist and she smiles back, pleased that she has been so helpful. Morten repeats the directions as he's told them, for me to write down, translating a word here and there into Norwegian for me, as my English is obviously weaker than his. I nod and write, nod and write. He asks if he can get the information over the phone and is told he can't because there's a one-dollar charge. He asks how long the drive will take and learns that it'll be under fifteen minutes.

"Thank you very much. *Takk skal du ha*," Morten says to the receptionist, pushing the phone back her way with a little bow.

"You're very welcome," she says, unable to take her eyes off him.

He waves, I wave, and we walk out the door.

Going down the stairs to the sidewalk, I say, "I'm pretty sure she would have said yes if I had asked her to borrow the phone without all the pretending."

"Maybe. Maybe," he says. "Probably. But pretending is so fun!"

We head east out of Manchester, around the back of the library. The buildings soon become residential, and then the roads are again tree-lined.

"This could easily be Norway," Morten says.

"Hmm."

"Let me think. Going east out of Oslo? There's more stone on the sides. We had to cut more stone to make our way through. But the road is like this. The trees."

He studies the map and guides me to a turnoff that will take us north over the top of a lake.

"Massabesic," he pronounces carefully. "What kind of name is that?"

"Native American, no doubt. Like Massachusetts."

I can see Morten shaking his head in my peripheral vision. "Honestly," he says, "who the hell did you think you were, smashing a city, a city named Manchester, on top of a Native American place?"

"I doubt it started out as a city," I say, then add, "Not that that's any justification."

"None at all."

After a moment I say, "You'll excuse the Vikings because they only massacred white people?"

"The Vikings are very often misrepresented."

No doubt he's right, but I don't think it's debated that they raided and pillaged and colonized. After my first few trips to Norway I developed a little theory. It was so hard to equate the reticent, hospitable people I was meeting with the legendary warring traders, that I figured that when the Vikings raised the battle cry and called on everyone to take up weapons and board their boats, only the really belligerent ones followed all the way through with it. The gentle ones stayed home and populated the land with more gentle ones.

Morten bucks that trend a bit, though.

"Ha! Now we could be in Denmark!" he says, pointing at a farmhouse painted red.

The houses of Auburn are very spread out, each surrounded by cleared land or woods. Which one sheltered my boys? Was it near the road, or back in the trees? We pass a sign for a school and soon we also see the sign for the post office, which sits well back in a pond of tarmac that is covered in tangled black squiggles showing repairs after frost heave upon frost heave.

Entering the building, I'm determined to be the one doing the talking, and even the sweet-talking if need be, but inside there is one person behind a counter meant for two, and that person is a young man. I hadn't imagined that, but of course Morten knew, having talked to him on the phone. Does Morten sense my hesitation? He looks at me and raises his eyebrows in a "Shall I?" expression. I nod, and get the notebook out of my jacket pocket, opening it to the right page.

"Hallo," Morten says as he approaches the counter. The young man, unremarkable in any way except for the heavy red frames of his eyeglasses, asks how he can help, without a smile.

"Well, we were exchange students here a long time ago and I just went to the last address where my host sister was living but she has moved. So I am wondering if you have a forwarding address for her."

"When did she move?"

"I don't know."

"When did you last hear from her from that address?"

"Maybe two, three years ago?"

"Are you sure she wants to see you?"

I wouldn't have any idea what to say to that, but Morten broadens rather than bristles. "Ha ha! What a good question. Maybe I am too . . . what is the word?" He turns to me and asks a question in Norwegian and I open my mouth like a fish and fortunately he jumps back in with "Conceited!", snapping his fingers. "Yes, I must be too conceited to imagine she wouldn't want to see me."

After a moment the young man says, "But what if she doesn't?"

"Well, then she won't see me, will she? Because she has moved away. But I still need the address because I want to send her a Christmas card."

The young man relaxes a smidge, but says, "If she moved away that long ago the order might not be here anymore."

"But you'll check?"

He shrugs. "Okay. It'll cost a dollar."

"Okay."

The young man turns around to a bank of wide file drawers and digs around in them. He digs for long enough for me to feel like I want to consider the padded envelope options arrayed on the shelves at the end of the room, but I follow Morten's lead and watch the search. For someone who seemed set against it, the young man is doing a very thorough job. Eventually he stands up straight again and comes back to the counter with a four-by-six card in his hands. Looking at it he says, "Want a photocopy? Or you can just write it down."

"Is there a price difference?" Morten asks.

"Nope."

"I'll take the photocopy, then."

"One dollar."

Both Morten and I reach for our wallets, but he stops me with a hand and puts a dollar on the counter. When the young man is at the machine, it's all I can do not to grab the copy from him. Once he has put it on the counter, Morten picks it up and considers it. I lean over to look too.

"Hamden, Connecticut," Morten says.

"For a while, anyway," the young man says. "You might get your Christmas card back if she's moved again."

"Or if she doesn't want to see me," Morten lobs back, folding the copy in two and slipping it into an inside pocket. The young man cracks a smile.

"Thanks," says Morten as we turn toward the door.

"*Takk skal du ha,*" I say with a wave.

"Okay, sure," says the young man.

Once the door has closed behind us Morten claps me on the back. "*Takk skal du ha!*" he says. "*Takk skal du* fucking *ha!*"

SIX

The doors swing open for one, two, three, four people, and then for Liv, looking pale and small, pulling her suitcase, casting unusually timid eyes around the waiting room. She normally rushes straight to me, but today she stops. I attribute this uncertainty to fatigue and rush forward myself, calling her name. She looks at me closely, almost squinting. I don't know this look. It should slow me down but I ignore it because I can't interpret it, or maybe I don't want to. I hug her and kiss her soft pale hair, and then her lips, which are slack. I decide she's tired. I guide her away from the doors and stop. "Do you need anything to eat before we get in the car, or to drink?" I ask her, and she looks at me, but her face is worried. She's clearly not trying to decide if she's thirsty.

"Livvie?"

Liv closes her eyes and sighs. She looks like she's trying not to cry. I take her gently by the shoulders. "Liv," I say. I say it again, louder, and Liv opens her eyes. "Say something, Livvie."

"I'm sorry," she says. "I just . . ." Tears spill down her cheeks.

I wrap my arms around her, and she rests her head on my shoulder, but she's still got her arms down by her sides. I pat her until it starts feeling sort of embarrassing that she hasn't moved her arms, so I let go and step back a little.

"What happened?" I ask her gently.

"I don't know."

"Why weren't you on the plane, though?"

She shakes her head then lets it hang down. "I don't know."

"Did you not want to come back?"

"Can we go home please?"

"Of course. Sorry."

I take the handle of her bag and we walk a few paces toward the exit before she stops again. I turn to look at her and something tells me not to move, because I might frighten her away, like a rabbit.

She speaks to me across the space.

"You are my husband?"

My mouth goes completely dry. "I am," I say carefully.

She says nothing.

"Do you remember me?"

Liv shakes her head, and her shoulders sag. She looks completely defeated. People continue to come out of the exit, some striding forward with their carry-on luggage, others drifting around until they are found and welcomed and guided. They swirl around us, around Liv, who looks like she'd have trouble moving in any direction at all. She says something, and I move closer, bending down to get closer to her mouth. "What was that?"

"I thought I would," Liv repeats.

"Not at all? You don't know who I am at all?"

"I do not."

We leave the terminal and take the pedestrian crossing that leads to the parking lot. Normally we'd be telling each other our pent-up stories on the way to the car, but Liv is quiet. I find my questions are too big to be asked while dragging her luggage, trying to read her face, getting us where we need to go. Once her suitcase is in the trunk and we're both belted in, I turn to her. She remains staring straight ahead.

"Liv," I say, my mouth still dry. I have to talk. I have to ask her something, just in case she can answer now. I need to know if she can answer now. "Where were you?"

When she looks at me she blinks, but it's not an opening. She still doesn't say anything.

This is happening.

We drive away from the airport. I'm heading for Brockton Hospital, where Noriko works.

It doesn't feel like I'm sitting next to Liv. I'm not getting the usual Liv vibe at all. She's hunched where she normally sits up straight or turns in her seat to look at me. She's staring out the window, but doesn't comment on anything. She seems frightened, like some sort of shell-shocked refugee. I'm quiet for as long as I can stand, and then I say, "You recognized your suitcase. That's good."

"It had my name on it."

"Oh. You looked at the names on all the suitcases?"

"No. No. It was in my room at the hotel in Oslo, and it had my name on it. I remembered it from the hotel."

"Which hotel?"

She looks over at me. "What do you mean?"

"You checked out of the Bondeheimen and then spent another night in Oslo after that."

She drops her head and rubs her temples.

"My poor Livvie. I'm surprised you came home at all, not remembering me."

"What else was there?" she says. "I couldn't reach my mother. And I had a husband. That is what I knew."

"Amnesia?" repeats the woman at a computer when I tell her why we've come to A&E.

I nod.

"Since?"

I look at Liv. Liv raises her shoulders and they stay up, so I answer. "Three days, maybe four."

She looks at Liv for confirmation, blue eyes to blue eyes. Liv nods.

"Have you forgotten everything?"

"No," Liv says.

"So should I give you the form to fill out, or him?"

"Him," Liv says.

While I fill out as much as I know of Liv's medical history and insurance details, Liv answers the woman's questions, tells her she doesn't have a headache, no, doesn't think she has hit her head, but yes, she's tired, she just got off a plane. There's a pause, so I look at the woman and she's looking at me for confirmation.

"Yes. We've come straight from the airport."

The woman nods. "Okay. Take a seat. Someone will be with you soon to sort out what tests will be done."

Fortunately, the chairs closest to the reception area are empty. We can sit with our backs to the handful of other waiting people — young and alone, old and alone, old and with family. One of them belches and sighs.

"Have I been here before?" Liv asks.

"No. You've been very healthy."

"Sometimes I must be sick."

"Well, yeah, you had bronchitis a few years ago. But there haven't been any emergencies."

We watch people in scrubs moving from place to place, meeting for a few words then moving again, like ants passing information as they cross paths. Every time one of them talks to the blond in blue I think they're being told about us and will come over, but it doesn't happen right away.

"I had chicken pox when I was little," Liv says after a while.

"That's hard to forget, isn't it?"

She smiles, for the first time. "Impossible," she agrees. "For the mother also. How terrible it must be to watch."

"I bet."

"I have scars," she says.

"I know," I say, startling her into looking at me, and she blushes.

"Oh my God I'm sorry," I say. "Did that sound creepy? That must have sounded so creepy. I didn't mean to make you —"

"It's okay," Liv says. "I don't think I know what creepy means."

"Oh. It's like yucky. Um, uncomfortable."

"Oh. Anyway, you were just saying it. It's, God, I wish I could just vomit. I feel so strange I want to vomit and make it go away. You know where my scars are. God."

I hope someone comes soon. Someone does, but to talk to people behind us, and we have another several minutes of wondering what's going on behind the curtains drawn between the beds off to our right. "Mahalia?" someone back there says. "Mahalia? Hello Mahalia, my name is Doctor Sanchez. Mahalia?" Her voice drops again, maybe to direct her colleagues. I keep thinking I've got to get to a phone and call Morten, but I'm afraid to leave Liv's side. A waft of air announces the man who appears in front of us, and we look up. He is as narrow and handsome as an Ethiopian runner.

"Svendsen?" he asks, and doesn't look like he's going to bend down, so I stand up and Liv follows. "Okay," he says in a strong Massachusetts accent, putting his clipboard under an arm, "I'm your physician's assistant. I'm just going to take your hands for a second." He lifts Liv's hands with his gloved ones. "Pretty cold," he says, and turns them over to look at her fingertips. "Do you feel breathless?"

She shakes her head.

"We're going to test your oxygen levels anyway. Come with me."

We walk behind him to an empty bed, where he has her sit and takes her temperature. Normal. He asks her to push up the left sleeve of her sweater and takes her blood pressure, and her pulse, which he says are fine, and then tells us they need to do blood work and a tox screen as he slides a needle into a vein in her arm and snaps vial after vial onto it. "Have you been partying?" he asks.

"I don't think so," Liv says.

"It's unlikely," I say.

"Not a big drinker, then?"

Liv looks at me. I smile at her. "No."

"It can be hidden," says the PA.

The sound of the vials clicking together is a nice sound, like backgammon checkers. Then there's a dull thumping and Doctor Sanchez is saying "Okay, okay, okay Mahalia, okay."

"I'm gonna get the lab work started on these. Then I'll come get you for a CT scan."

"Any idea how long we'll be waiting for that?"

"Not really. Have a seat."

There's another waiting area outside medical imaging – three navy-blue chairs under a photograph of a lighthouse at the end of a green peninsula. Here we're the only ones waiting, and this time the practitioner crouches down in front of Liv with a squeak of her rubber-soled shoes. Maybe she's used to people hanging their heads. Her hair is deeply black. It would be attractively shiny in better light.

"I'm Monica," she says, "and I'll be doing your CT scan. Can I just double check this information?" She's holding a printed sheet of paper. Liv nods. "Liv Svendsen?" Liv nods again, as do I. "Date of birth?"

"November 22nd, 1960."

"Oh! Three days ago!" Monica says.

Liv sits up a bit. "Oh!"

"Happy birthday," Monica says.

"Thank you," Liv says.

"Shall we go in?"

We all stand up, and I ask how long the scan takes.

"Ten minutes or so?" Monica answers.

"Does it hurt?" Liv asks.

"Not at all. You just lie down, and you won't feel a thing."

"I'm going to make a call," I say to them both.

Liv nods. Monica says, "Sure."

I watch the big door close behind them and then jog back to A&E where I saw a phone. I dial my home number and wait for Morten to answer. The wall to the left of the phone is discolored at about five feet. People leaning with a hand on the wall while they talk? Or their head?

"Hello?" says Morten.

"Morten, it's Leo."

"Why aren't you here? Did she not arrive again?"

His brusqueness irks me. "No, she did, but I'm calling from the hospital."

"What?"

"We don't know what has happened, but she's lost some memory."

"She *what*?"

"She's lost some memory."

"Of what?"

"There's a lot I don't know yet, okay? She's upset and I don't want to ask a lot of questions."

"Okay, yes, okay. So what's happening?"

"They're testing her blood, and she's having a CT scan of her head now."

Morten is silent. So am I. Then he says, "Dinner will be waiting. It can be eaten any time."

"That's great. Thanks a lot." I regret being irritated. I want to say, "It's good you're here," but I don't do it. Instead I say, "The scan takes about ten minutes, but we'll have to wait for the results of everything."

"Of course," he says.

"Make yourself at home," I tell him, and he laughs. "Why are you laughing?"

"If you could see me," he says. "I'm wearing a polka dot apron."

I can easily imagine him moving confidently around my kitchen, amusing himself. The tapes of Liv's apron must only barely meet behind him.

"Well," I say, "I've got to get back."

"Do what you need to," he says, warmly now. "I'll be here."

Jogging back to medical imaging — needlessly, but I need to burn up adrenalin — I try to imagine the black-and-white images of the inside of Liv's head that Monica is producing. I've never seen a CT scan in real life, but I know they show the head from the top. Cross sections. Maybe I've seen them on TV. A pregnant colleague brought an ultrasound scan of her fetus in to work once. As I sit and wait, the images converge in my mind, the two lobes of Liv's brain appearing as twin fetuses, their backs curved against the wall of her skull. I realize I'm imagining the inside of Marilyn's womb for the first time. I feel my face get hot. Marilyn is the mother of my children. They'd be seven years old now. I think I have the right to imagine them inside her, but it feels like I'm betraying Liv by doing so.

Until recently I haven't thought much about them. Well, in the beginning I did. I imagined their birth, their shocking, shiny, possibly identical nakedness, their need to be detached from their mother, their need to be cleaned, their need for absolutely everything. That's where my imagination ended. I never saw them upright and toddling in my mind. I never pictured them in clothes. But then Liv and I fought in a way we've never fought before, and her stubbornness about not having children triggered my curiosity. Maybe even my desire. Because now, I want to meet them. *The boys*, I say to myself tentatively. *My boys*.

When I met Marilyn, my mother was recently dead and I had been doing nothing but teaching for over a year. I hadn't been on a date, hadn't taken a trip, hadn't even had a haircut. I was a very shaggy dog when I finally decided to take up an activity and strayed into her etching class one January evening. By the time I had strayed to her apartment and stumbled into her bedroom, the shaggy dog was gone, replaced by a slobbery one. Between classes I would starve for her, and doodle pictures of her full lips, and then feel like an idiot. Halfway through class she'd pass behind me and her long, heavy braid would brush my shoulder and I would cease to exist except for an inch of skin's memory of the weight of her hair.

And then, at the end of the semester, not even four months after we had met, she left. No note, no call. The key I had to her faculty apartment still worked, but the apartment was empty of her things except for a gum wrapper in a dusty corner. Big Red. Sometimes her tongue stung mine because of it. The university personnel office told me they had no forwarding information whatsoever. The art department said the same. I stood in the office feeling unzipped in the most embarrassing way. The kindly secretary took pity on me. "Maybe she'll get in touch with us," she said, "when she realizes she needs something. I'll let you know."

Marilyn had never told me she loved me, but she had seemed happy. Ecstatic, even, at moments. I had assumed I was part of that. Well, I was, but not for the reasons I had imagined. I've never played emotional games, and I didn't have it in me to go after her. I zipped myself back up instead.

I hadn't loved her either, I realized. I had been in thrall. Pussy-whipped, I told myself. What an idiot. Let it go.

I met Liv in the classical section of a music store that winter. She was so small and so heavily bundled up that I'm sure I wouldn't have noticed her if it hadn't been for her naked hands. I stared openly at Liv's expressive pink fingers as they walked on their clean nails across the tops of the cassettes.

"Any recommendations?" I asked.

She looked up smiling, unwary, and then down again. I noticed she was filing through the M's. "Usually Mozart," she said. "But I was just trying to get my thoughts organized at the office, and the radio was playing something so beautiful by Mendelssohn that I couldn't work. I had to stop and listen." This was the most interesting thing anyone had said to me in months. I watched her carefully as she pulled out a cassette and considered the selections listed on the back, then returned it. I registered her pixie-like profile. "What are *you* looking for?" she asked, pulling out another cassette.

Suddenly I wanted to interest her as well. Suddenly there was so much I wanted to tell her. "Something like spring," I said. "No dark colors. Daisies. Ice melting . . . flies . . . bees."

"Try Vivaldi's guitar concertos," she said seriously. "Or Claude Bolling. Have you listened to them?" I shook my delighted head. "Then listen to both," she said, and nodded at the Mendelssohn cassette in her hand, indicating that she had made the right choice for herself as well.

After spending our money and pocketing our music we sat down for coffee together.

"Why no dark colors?" she asked.

"Well, I just . . . I recently lost . . ." I forced myself to look across into her unblinking blue eyes. I changed my answer. "I recently lost my mother," I told her.

She drew me out with positive questions and appeared to enjoy my childhood anecdotes. Our coffee together turned into the memorial service I had never organized for my mother.

It was back in the art department a few months into my relationship with Liv that I learned about the twins. I was standing by the secretary's desk, in about the same place as I had been when she'd told me she didn't know how to reach Marilyn. She was helping me get some handouts photocopied. While I waited I picked up the postcard propped against her pen mug and turned it over to ascertain if it was photography or realism. It was a painting, by Richard Estes. I recognized the handwriting of the message. Signed Marilyn. The secretary was still photocopying. I read: "Twin boys born! Both healthy! And hungry! More soon!" Postmarked Auburn, NH. Dated December. I replaced it quickly and had a couple of seconds to do the math. Marilyn had left in May. May to December was seven months. The secretary handed me the photocopies. The top and bottom ones stuck to my sweaty hands. I had to stop in the hallway and lean against the wall. Twin boys born. Seven months. Seven months. They could have been premature. If they weren't mine, they would have had to have been conceived in May. Or after May. In which case, what were the chances of premature twins being born so healthy? They would have been tiny. How else might they not be mine? Did Marilyn have other partners when she was with me? I didn't think so. We spent most of our free time together, but you can't be sure. I used a condom, she used a diaphragm, until we decided we trusted each other to be monogamous and ditched the condom. Kept the diaphragm. I believed. They might not be mine. But they might be mine. Light-headed, I made my way back to my classroom and put the photocopies on a shelf. I left the college and drove to my apartment on automatic pilot.

I believed the twins were mine by the time I got home, because that explained both Marilyn's ardor – I'd never been found ardor-worthy before – and her disappearance. She wanted kids. Alone.

So, until otherwise convinced, I had two-month-old twin boys. But I was in love with Liv, and she was about to move in with me. We had talked about kids, and she seemed absolutely terrified by the idea. She would shudder if I brought it up. There's time, I'd thought. We can come back to it, I'd thought. So I mentally put the postcard away. It wasn't so hard to do, as long as I reminded myself from time to time that they *might* not be mine. I avoided the departmental office. If I didn't think about the postcard, it didn't exist. The boys didn't. Only Liv and I did, and we were happy.

I hear the imaging room door open and turn to see Liv come out followed by a smiling Monica. I stand up and Monica says, "You'll have to wait for the doctor's confirmation, but her brain looks fine to me. There's no sign of hemorrhage, nothing strange."

"There must be," Liv says dully.

"Well, yes, but not because of any identifiable physical change to the brain. That's really good."

"Is it?" I say.

"Memories lost from a physical emergency are more difficult to recover."

"I see."

"Yup. So you can go back to the main waiting area and you'll be called when your blood work is done. Okay? Any questions?"

I look at Liv, who shakes her head.

"Know your way back?" Monica asks me, and I say, "Yup," at the same time as Liv says, "I hope there is one."

Monica squeezes Liv's arm. "Baby steps," she says, and we walk away from the lighthouse, back toward Mahalia and the PA who didn't tell us his name.

Liv is asleep across three chairs when the PA comes back to us about 90 minutes later. It's nearly ten p.m. I've called Morten again. I've had a Mars bar. I've suffered through the arrival and departure of a heavily tattooed woman with what I chose to believe was food poisoning rather than an overdose. It calmed me to watch Liv sleep with my jacket under her head.

"Wakey wakey," says the PA, and I pat Liv on the shoulder. She's so deeply asleep I have to speak right in her ear and pull her up to a sitting position.

"Come on back over here," the PA says, and returns to the curtained bed, leaving me to remind the still blurry Liv where we are and to get her on her feet.

"Okay," the PA says. "Looks good, looks good. Nothing out of the ordinary."

"You saw the CT scan too?"

"Yeah. Good stuff."

"So what's wrong with her?"

Liv is blinking in a way that gives me sympathetic sand in my own eyes.

"You'll have to consult a psychiatrist, I think."

"These tests are a hundred percent conclusive?"

He gives me a sharp look, and then remembers he shouldn't do that. "We can set you up with a neurologist," he says, "but I'd say you can safely go home and get her some rest and see if it clears up."

"What, like a rash?"

"Yeah, actually. Those can be psychological too. I see those all the time. Give it a few days."

I look at Liv, who is looking at me, waiting for me to finish the conversation with the PA. "So," I say, "it's safe to go home."

"Yes," he says. "If there's no improvement in a few days, then I'd contact psychiatry here."

We thank him, and we stop to confirm payment details, and I call Morten one more time to let him know we'll be home in about 20 minutes. I haven't told Liv whom I'm calling. I can't see my way into it until we've pulled into the driveway. Liv sits up and looks around, giving me a renewed look of bewilderment and helplessness. If I photographed it, I wouldn't be able to look at the photo again. "I don't remember this house," she says.

"Shall we see what happens inside?"

She nods bravely.

As I close the trunk after pulling out her luggage, I stop our forward motion by saying, "Liv, Morten's here."

"Morten?"

"Your brother. Your half-brother."

She tips her head, as if hoping to sense a dribble of memory like water trapped in an ear after swimming. "I have a half-brother?"

"Apparently."

"What's he like?"

"Oh, well," I search the sky, disappointed. Neither of us can help each other yet. It's like when someone asks you how to get somewhere and you're in your town but a different part of town than you're used to, and you can't direct them. You want to say, "This *is* where I live, though." I tell her, "I don't know where to start. I thought you might be able to fill me in a little, since you've never mentioned him to me."

"I have no idea," she says. "What's he doing here?"

"He came for your birthday."

"Oh."

"And I've invited him for Thanksgiving. I thought you'd be able to tell me who he was, and we could uninvite him if you wanted."

"Oh."

"Maybe I shouldn't have done that."

She shrugs. "I don't know."

"Well, he should have prepared dinner for us."

"I'm starving," she says, so I start picking up her bags, but she doesn't move yet. She's staring at me.

"How shall we handle this?" I ask her as I start to really feel the cold.

"How do we usually handle things?"

I clear my throat. "Pretty much straight on, with, um, timid good humor. How's that?"

"Okay," she says. "Okay, Leo."

We open the door. At the sound Morten stops arranging food on the table and stands up straight to smooth his cords.

"Liv! *Hei!*" he says.

Liv doesn't speak, just takes him.

Morten shoots me a questioning glance. I raise my shoulders; we're together in the dark now.

We wait. I look from her to him and back. She's blinking rapidly, he's unblinking. She stops blinking, but says nothing.

"Well," says Morten, clapping his hands and rubbing them together like a tour guide, "Shall we eat? We can get reacquainted over the meal, no?"

We strip off our coats, pull out chairs, reach for knives and fill our plates. Morten has covered the table with platters of ham and cheese, little bowls of caviar and sour cream, rye bread on a cutting board, fresh pink shrimp on rounds of toast surrounded by cherry tomatoes and parsley. Morten inquires, as if we had been conversing smoothly rather than stumbling from brick wall to brick wall, "And your mother? How was Karin?"

Liv looks to me. "Was I visiting my mother?"

I nod apologetically.

"I thought I would at least remember home when I arrived," she says.

"Still nothing?"

She shakes her head.

Morten lifts his plate of open-faced sandwiches. "Do you remember *smørbrød*?"

Liv smiles. "Yes," she says. We all loosen up a little, eat another few mouthfuls, and then suddenly Liv drops her hands to her lap. "I am so tired," she tells us.

"Of course you are." I jump up, pick up her bags. She hasn't moved. I put the bags down again and pull her chair out gently. Morten's face is tense, fascinated, as I lead Liv out of the kitchen.

Liv stands in the space between our bedroom door and the bed. She's swaying slightly. After looking at the bed for a long moment, she looks around the room, then back at the bed. I have stayed behind her. I thought she might walk around the room, but her feet are rooted. I come to stand next to her, and now we're both staring at the bed and its faded turquoise bedspread. "I can sleep on the couch," I say.

She nods, and I feel awful. It will feel very wrong sleeping downstairs, with both Morten and Liv upstairs, like it's their house, not Liv's and mine. I can't imagine myself actually sleeping. I have to try really hard to put myself in her shoes, to accept that everything she sees is unfamiliar to her, including me, to keep myself from saying that I'll be good and please can I sleep in our room too?

"Do you want me to leave you now?" I ask her instead. "Do you need anything? There's a cup in the bathroom if you want a drink of water."

She smiles at me. "I just need to sleep. Maybe in the morning I will remember."

"Maybe you will. Don't hesitate to wake me up in the night if you're, I don't know, afraid, or anything. Anything."

"Thank you," she says sadly.

I close the door behind me. I've never closed the bedroom door from the outside with Liv on the inside.

Morten is still at the table when I get back to the kitchen. He has cleared Liv's dinner things away, but has left my nearly full plate and his, which still has a few morsels on it. He's just sitting, with the fingers of one hand around the stem of his wine glass. I've seen him eat. He eats fast, with gusto. I can tell he has saved these morsels so we'll be seated at the table together for a while longer even though it's so late, even though I'm sure we both want to get to tomorrow as quickly as possible.

I sit.

"What do you think happened?" he asks me before taking a casual sip of wine, possibly to reduce the intensity of his look.

"Something bad, that's all I know." I put some food in my mouth.

"Necessarily?"

I move the food into my cheek to talk. "What else could it be?"

"They did every test they could?"

"I assume so."

"So maybe not."

"Okay, maybe not. We can consult a neurologist if we want. Or a psychiatrist."

He makes a sound, *pshurr*, and drinks again.

I chew and swallow. "Not a fan of psychiatrists, then?"

He shakes his head, dismissing the profession. "We'll sort this out."

I've eaten what I can. "I'm bushed," I say.

"She blinked a lot when she saw me," he says. "Did she blink a lot when she saw you?"

I think. "No, it was more of a squint."

He considers this. I want to think about it too. Alone. I get up and tear off some plastic wrap to cover my plate with before putting it in the fridge.

"I'll be on the couch," I tell him as he's draining his glass.

"No!" he says. "Take the guest room!"

"Not tonight," I say. "I've told her I'll be down here, so I better be down here."

He gazes at me for a moment, and then he says, "You're a nice man."

It's true. I know I'm nice. So I say, "Takes one to know one," quite cheerfully, as I leave the kitchen.

I'm halfway through the living room when I hear him respond: "No, it doesn't."

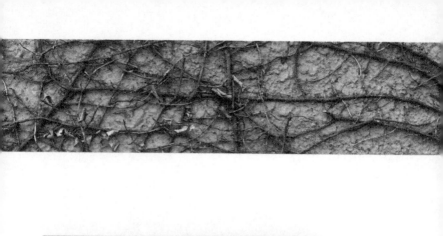

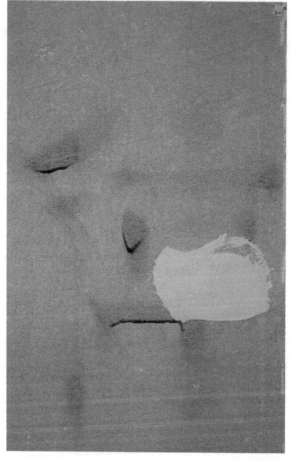

SEVEN

I try to stay awake to monitor the sounds from upstairs, and then I wake up without realizing I've slept. Liv is in front of me bathed in sunlight. I forgot to pull down the shades when I went to bed on the couch.

"Oh good," she says.

I sit up. "How are you?"

"I'm glad it's daytime. It feels more real."

"You found your pajamas."

She looks at the set I bought her a few birthdays before: red, white and blue tartan. The colors of the Norwegian flag, as well as the American flag. "I found pajamas, anyway. You slept in your clothes?"

"In case of emergency, I guess." I shrug, feeling shy. She's staring at me. Even lovers don't usually stare at each other for as long as she's staring at me.

"Hungry?" I ask.

"I was a few hours ago, but not now."

"You could have come down."

She shakes her head. "Let's go for a walk."

"Okay. Morten too?"

She thinks for a moment. "No."

I'm relieved. "Okay. Sure."

"I'll change my clothes," she says, heading upstairs, and I tidy up the couch feeling optimistic. I also make her a piece of toast and spread it with butter and jam that I'll insist she eat before we got out.

Outside it is bright and crisp.

"Slow down, please," she says.

I apologize and adjust my pace to hers. She stops and does a slow three-sixty. I decide not to ask her if she recognizes anything. She'll tell me if she does, I imagine. When she starts walking again I follow, my earlier buoyancy deflating. We pass a house with a large carved pumpkin on the steps. Three weeks after Halloween, it looks deflated too.

"What is Thanksgiving like?" Liv asks.

"Well, it's a holiday where —"

"No, I mean, what do we do?"

"You remember what Thanksgiving is?"

She looks surprised. "I guess so. Well, I've heard of it."

Someone in a house on the right is playing the piano and the regularity of the scales is comforting. Everything takes practice. "Well, there's just the two of us . . ."

"Why?"

I wonder if I'm brave enough to bring up our childlessness, and then say, "My parents are both dead, so they can't join us."

"Oh! I'm so sorry!"

"It's fine. And I'm an only child."

"Me too!" She says it as if we've just met, as if we're on a first date, finding out how similar we are.

"Really?" I reply. "What about Morten?"

She stops walking, and her face clouds over. I regret the question and I change the subject. "We don't have kids," I say.

"That's obvious," she says.

I laugh.

"Why don't we have kids, Leo?"

I can't decide how to word it.

"You can tell me later," Liv says, moving again. "Maybe I don't need to know right now."

We kick at the dry leaves as we walk.

She speaks again. "So, we don't have enough family . . . we don't eat enough to have turkey at Thanksgiving, is that right?"

"Yes," I say, "that's exactly it." She seems to understand my effort to communicate carefully. To me this means she must remember me. I want to hug her. I start whistling "Joy to the World" instead. At the next corner Liv stops and stares across the street at the house I pointed out to Morten just the day before. It is heavily bedecked with lights and long streamers of plastic holly, and Santas in three different sizes wave from the front yard. I stop whistling.

"What do we usually do at Christmas?" Liv asks.

I flash back to last Christmas Eve. Liv and I sat by the tree drinking spiced wine, poking at the presents with the toes of our slippers. I mentioned, probably not for the first time in our relationship, how simple and quiet Christmas had been when I was growing up. I always got one present, and it was always exactly what I wanted. But I liked the idea of piles of gifts and paper being ripped off and left all over the floor. "Wouldn't that be nice?" I had asked Liv.

"I'm not so sure."

"Why not? What's not to like about a little excess at Christmas time?"

"It's not the excess, Leo. It's the kids." She wouldn't look at me.

"What kids?"

"Don't pretend you don't understand. You want kids. You want kids opening lots of presents."

"Okay! I seem to want kids! Why don't you?"

She stopped the rhythm of the conversation to think. She looked worried but all she said was, "Maybe it's fear."

"Fear of what?"

Instead of answering she suddenly put on a bright face. I thought she'd had a revelation and I was going to learn something, but she was just changing the subject. "Let's open our presents!" she said.

"Wait a sec, Livvie. I want to understand. Why won't you ever explain to this to me? Did something happen to you?"

"You know what I've never understood, Leo?"

"What?"

"Why people don't leave other people's decisions alone."

"But I'm your husband. How can these questions be inappropriate?" The wine had made my cheeks warm, and now the confusion made them burn.

"I was feeling so lovely until you asked them."

"So let's get to the bottom of it. Get it done. What's so difficult? Why is there no answer?"

She looked at me. I had never seen her look so threatening. Her eyes were like ice. "Because there isn't."

"Well, merry Christmas," I said childishly, and then stupidly tried to pull myself off the floor with one of the tree's lower branches. I hadn't meant to pull the tree over. I hadn't meant to fight back like this. But having begun, I continued, leaving the room as the tree bounced and tinkled on its side, and then leaving the house.

I stomped around the neighborhood until stomping felt dumb. When I got home, the now undecorated tree was standing outside by the back steps, and Liv wasn't in the living room. I found her upstairs in bed, with our presents beside her.

"Let's open our presents," she said again, pleading this time. She looked like she regretted ejecting the Christmas tree. I certainly regretted walking out. I wanted Liv more than I wanted children with Liv. But I did want children with Liv, and somehow I needed an answer. But this time I let her change the subject. We gave and received, and then we folded the wrapping paper away. I changed and climbed into bed, and we fell asleep hugging. Christmas and that particular conversation were over.

Now, staring at the garishly decorated house, I ask Liv, "Do you remember last Christmas?"

"No," she says. "Did we have a nice one?"

I look down into her completely open face. "It was okay," I say.

We find Morten in the living room with Mozart. He has his feet up, eyes closed, elbows on the arms of the chair, the tips of his fingers lightly pressed together. This man has no trouble finding comfortable positions for himself. His body is so large, but so tidy. I imagine that there is absolutely nothing in his handsome nasal passages to inhibit their superlative functioning. I imagine his bowels chugging everything through healthily. He opens his eyes.

Liv has stopped rubbing her cold hands together to listen to the music. She tips her head like a little dog with a question. Morten watches her, unblinking. "When you are ready to talk about our family," he tells her quietly, deliberately, "just say the word."

She hasn't moved. Finally she shakes her head. "I have to go back to bed." I follow her to the stairs but she waves me away.

Back in the living room, Morten is sitting up now, feet on the floor, face sharp and bright. "When shall we go get the turkey?" he asks me, as if food might be anywhere on my mind. I breathe out heavily through my nose. The phone rings in the kitchen. It's Noriko.

"How is she?"

"She's still confused. And exhausted."

"But she's home, right? I looked at her file."

"Yes. Nothing obviously wrong."

"Other than in her behavior."

"Yeah. But that could change. They said leave it a few days."

"Do you think she'd talk to me?"

"Probably. But it would be like talking to a stranger."

"I've never gone this long without talking to her. Wow. I can only imagine how *you* must feel."

"It's certainly hard to describe."

"Try to take it minute by minute."

The concern in her voice is very welcome. I imagine having her around and feel my burden lightened. "Hey," I say, "what are you doing at Thanksgiving?"

"Oh, you know. I'll work that day, then I'll sit around in the evening eating popcorn like on any other evening, and wish my parents were more American, or I were more

Japanese, so that I could stop feeling so torn. I'd like either not to want a turkey dinner, or to have it. Every year it's the same."

"Come to our house."

"Leo. Darling. My first-born child is yours."

I eat lunch with Morten, and when I'm washing our plates I look out the window. The weather's changing but there's still a little bit of sun. I turn around and say, "Soccer?"

Morten jumps up out of his chair.

We play through the leaves that never got raked into bags. They're drier now. Sometimes the ball disappears. Morten is tricky, leading me on a chase around and around the house, until slowly I begin to dominate the game. He lets me. I appear to run him ragged, and leap around like Rocky Balboa when he leans over with his hands on his knees and heaves his belly in and out in fake fatigue.

"You win," he says.

Inside I take off my shoes. Morten has decided to stay outside and really put an end to the raking job. I stroll into the living room, wondering what is supposed to happen next, and I hear the TV on upstairs.

In the bedroom, Liv is sitting like a small child in a mess of bed covers, cross-legged, spine rounded, entranced. She speaks to me but her eyes never leave the screen. "Did I watch this show before?"

I step closer to the bed and look at the TV. I've never seen the show, but it is recognizably mediocre, and the laugh track is absurdly clumsy.

"No."

"But it's so funny."

I watch the colors flicker over her delighted face. "I'm going out to get us some food before Morten has time to lay on another huge meal," I tell her. "Anything you particularly want?"

Commercials have started and she tears her gaze from the screen. "What do I usually want?"

"You're totally unpredictable."

She looks pleased, then disappointed. "How to decide, then?"

"Greek?"

"I'll try it."

"You've had it millions of times."

A pause as she stares at the TV again. "Then I'll probably like it." Another pause. A smile meant for me, but directed at the TV. "Thanks."

I slide my car keys off the dresser. Just as I step out into the hall she says, "The commercials are funny too, aren't they?"

Morten is still raking when I pull out of the driveway, although by now it's getting dark. When I pull back in forty minutes later the house is blazing with lights.

"We're in here," Morten calls from the living room when he hears me come in, so I grab forks, napkins, and plates, and take the food through. Liv is walking slowly beside the bookshelves, dragging a finger along the titles as she reads each one. Morten has the tips of his fingers together again. I raise my eyebrows at him hopefully. He shakes his head.

Liv sits on the floor by the coffee table and I join her. "I can't remember ever being this hungry," she says, helping me take the Styrofoam containers from the brown paper bag.

Unrehearsed, Morten and I start heaping food on her

plate, met with giggles of appreciation. As we serve ourselves Liv suddenly says, "I'd really like to see my mother."

This isn't something she's ever said before. Karin calls a few times a month, and Liv calls her from time to time, usually when she needs something done in Norway, but she's always seemed to tolerate her mother more than cherish her. "We're Norwegian," she tells me if I comment on it. "We're not expressive like you."

"We can call her," I say. Liv smiles and puts a piece of pita dripping with taramasalata in her mouth, and I'm surprised by a twinge of arousal. I very deliberately cut my pita with my knife and fork as a distraction, and Morten says, "Wasn't your visit enough?"

Liv turns to me for guidance again, something she keeps doing, which continues to encourage me that deep down she remembers our connection. But it also makes me sad. She's so lost.

"You saw her in Norway," I tell her gently, "less than a week ago." She starts chewing again, with less energy. Morten and I eat too.

I don't know why Morten thinks to say what he says next, but it serves to improve all our moods. "Who here has broken a bone?" he asks.

Liv's head snaps up. "I have!" she says, grinning, less I think at the specific recollection than at the fact that she has been able to recollect.

"Which one?" asks Morten, and Liv holds out her wrist, and tells the story of being pulled over by her dog when she was eleven.

"I fell out of a tree," says Morten. "Broke my femur."

"How old were you?" Liv asks.

"Twenty-four," he says, at which of course we laugh, and

the meal takes off. Morten entertains us and we respond with disbelief, mock horror, and simple enjoyment. Morten says, "...at which point the old witch of a nurse tells me that ten stitches is nothing, and if I want to see some really impressive battle scars I could have a private tour in the staff room," and we laugh, and then I say, "Oh yeah, speaking of nurses, I invited Noriko for Thanksgiving."

"Who's Noriko?" asks Liv.

"She's our best friend. More American than I am, but her parents are too Japanese to bother with turkey. She lives with them. She's a hospital nurse."

Leaving Liv to think about that, I start clearing the refuse from the table. "Dessert, anyone? There's still cake."

"Do you think there's anything good on TV?" Liv asks.

"Nope," I say.

"Absolutely not," confirms Morten.

Liv looks down, thinks. "I'll just check."

EIGHT

When I wake up in the morning the TV is already on upstairs. This time I've slept in pajamas. Liv smiles weakly at me when I arrive in the bedroom and then continues flipping between morning news shows. She lands on a cartoon.

"Okay if I sit here?" I ask her, pointing to the corner of the bed. She nods without looking at me. I rub my eyes and try to focus. Pretty soon I'm giggling with her. I've never really watched cartoons.

When she finally gets up off the bed she bends over her open suitcase to pull out a turtleneck.

"You have a whole closet full of clothes, you know," I tell her. "Why don't you unpack?"

She goes into the bathroom and comes right back out again. Then she crosses to the closet and pulls it open, broadcasting such a strong sense of courage and determination that I wince internally as the door swings out.

After a long moment staring at her clothes, Liv reaches for the sleeve of a dress to inspect it. "This is nice."

"It's one of your favorites."

She shakes her head and moves on to another sleeve.

"Are you beginning to remember Morten?"

Another shake of the head. "I remember my mother," she says.

"Shall we call her? She'd be awake now. I'd like to see if she's home, actually. I've been trying to reach her for days."

"No," she says. "Not right now."

"Do you remember me today?" The question sits like an anvil on my chest and I can't breathe. The phone rings. I turn to reach over and answer, and when I turn back Liv is closing the bathroom door. It's her mother.

"Karin," I say warmly. "Speak of the devil."

"How is Liv? She's home now, *ja*?"

"Yes, she is."

"Good. Wonderful."

"I've been calling you every day, well mostly every night, Karin. I needed to reach you."

"Oh? Sorry! I was in Stavanger. Is there something wrong?"

"Liv seems to have had a shock at the end of her trip, in Oslo I think. Or, I don't know, maybe an accident? Whatever happened, she doesn't remember much."

"Not much about what?"

"She can't remember her life here."

"Oh no! Does she remember you?"

"No."

"Oh Leo! Your house?"

"No."

"Herself? Has she forgotten who she is?"

"No, fortunately. But she can't seem to retrieve any of her American life. Maybe some of her Norwegian life too."

"*Herregud!*"

I wait again.

"She remembers me, then?" she eventually asks.

"She remembers you, in the past."

"Only in the past?"

"Yes."

"How frightening!"

I can't tell from her voice if she means for Liv or for herself.

"Well, I think you can take heart," I say, wondering if I'm doing the right thing, "She doesn't remember Morten at all."

"Who is Morten?" she says, right away. A catch in her voice? I don't think so. "You have a dog now?"

"No, no. Liv's half-brother Morten."

In the long pause that follows I can hear her radio in the background. "There is no Morten in the family," she says.

"He knows who *you* are, though." I speak more quietly and more urgently. "I had never heard of him before he turned up at the back door. He said he got our address from you. He brought a cake for Liv."

"Nobody asked me for your address, Leo. Nobody. I would have told you. Please can I talk to her?"

"Let me ask." I put the receiver on the bedside table and knock on the bathroom door.

"Who is it?"

"It's your mother."

The door opens with a jerk. "You are not my mother."

"On the telephone. Would you like to speak with her?"

She shakes her head for a long time. Not just a quick left-right, but a determined shaking. She turns back to the mirror.

"You wanted to last night," I whisper.

This surprises her.

"Maybe if you heard her voice?"

"Maybe if I heard her voice I would go crazy." The door closes.

I sit on the edge of the bed. "I'm sorry, Karin."

"No?"

"Oh dear."

"Maybe tomorrow."

"Leo, I was thinking, what did the doctor say?"

"No obvious physical trauma. So, some sort of shock? We're supposed to wait a few days."

"And then?"

"Psychiatrist, I guess. Hypnotist?"

"This is too terrible!"

"Maybe it will resolve quickly."

"This man, Morten, what does he look like?"

"Blond hair, a bit curly, well built."

"Curly? Really curly? Or more waved?"

"Well, I guess, in between curly and wavy."

A third silence.

"So, she doesn't have a half-brother named Morten?"

"I don't know anyone at all named Morten."

"Then . . . ?"

"He must be a liar. I think I would make him go away. Yes. I would do that. You can call the police, make him go away."

"He says they played together as children."

"No."

"She didn't play with a boy she didn't know was her half-brother?"

"Leo, you are sounding crazy. She did not do that."

"But —"

"Okay," she interrupts. "I'll call again very soon. In between I will buy a plane ticket to Boston."

"Thank you. I could really use the help."

"Okay, we talk again."

"Okay."

"Okay. Make him go away, Leo. Bye."

After a long and truly blank moment I go to the window and open the curtains, dazzling myself. The sun, though low in the sky, shines brightly on the neighborhood, and on Morten, who is getting into his car. His windshield flashes as he pulls away from the curb. Karin knows who he is, I'm almost sure. She's lying, or Morten is. Or both of them are. The only thing I'm clear on is that Karin doesn't want Morten near Liv. I want him to come back, though, even if it's just to tell him to go away.

Liv and I start off slowly after breakfast with the least threatening of the photo albums: me, growing up. For the first few pages, I provide a running commentary, encouraged by Liv's nods, but I realize that she isn't actually engaging in the exercise, just being polite, as you would to someone you'd just met but liked. On the fifth or sixth page, I fall silent. We flip wordlessly through two more old albums of friends, other people's babies, and then she wants to see our wedding.

"Are you sure?"

"Just a few pages."

I retrieve the album and place it in her lap but remain standing. I feel like leaving the room, coming back later to hear the verdict, but I can't help craning my head around when she opens to the first photo, and my body follows. I sit, put an arm across the back of the couch, lean in. Liv smiles at the long-haired minister, at the horses lined up at the fence of the adjoining farm. For three pages we are both smiling.

"Who's that?"

"That's your second cousin, Olav."

"A man now!"

"What do you mean?"

"We used to climb trees together. He could jump from the highest branches." Pause. "I couldn't have imagined him ever growing that fat. Does he play the guitar well?"

"When the guitar is in tune, I'm sure he's excellent."

"Who's that?" She's growing bolder.

"That's Gundvor. I think she's your great-aunt."

"Yes. What a lot of lipstick."

"She's lovely. You have a wonderful family."

Liv stops smiling, taps a finger against Karin's face in a beautiful portrait of the two of them.

"Your mother," I say. They wear exactly the same short, soft hairstyle.

"I know," she says. "Just not with these little wrinkles. What is the story of the man who sleeps for years and then when he goes home everyone is gone, or old?"

"Rip Van Winkle?"

"Yes. Am I Rip Van Winkle?"

"No, Liv."

"Liv Van Winkle."

"No."

"Liv Van Wrinkle."

I laugh, but I feel I could actually cry. "You're not old, Liv."

She seems to shiver, and then looks back at the album. She turns a few more pages without seeing them, then closes it. She gets up and crosses to the stairs.

"TV?" I ask.

She nods and heads up.

. . .

In the darkroom, I pull down the photos that have dried and mix the solution to develop another roll. In my head, for a time, I hear echoes of Liv's voice. "Where's this?" "Who's that?" "What did he die of?"

Eventually I become absorbed. Near the end of the process I start to whistle. When I come back up, Morten is in the kitchen, broiling fish. He doesn't hear me behind him. I've become so used to how he always gets lunch organized – more than used to it; I'm thrilled by it – that it takes me a moment to remember that I'm supposed to tell him that Karen denies knowing anyone called Morten. He turns around to reach for an apple and sees me.

"Leo!" he says, "I got a job!"

"*What?* Where?"

"Here, actually."

"Here?"

"Yes."

"This suburb has a soccer team?"

He laughs. "Chapel Hill-Chauncy Hall does."

"Say what?"

"I got myself a low-paying job teaching P.E. and coaching high school soccer. Girls in the spring, boys in the fall. And a position with a new indoor league for the winter."

"Is that what you want?"

"I want to stay here and help you."

"Help me with what?"

"With Liv. And with your soccer skills. And," he adds, checking the fish under the broiler, "with lunch."

"It seems like a big step down, no?"

He shrugs. "I like it here. In Atlanta, I liked the job, but not the place, or the people. So that's only one out of the three important things. Here I like the place, and the people. Two out of three. Maybe I'll actually like the job too. I've already found a place to live."

"Wow! Where is the school?"

"Waltham."

"Okay, cool," I say. Waltham is about an hour away. "You'll move out soon?"

"As soon as possible, I promise," he says, smiling broadly, and sets to slicing the apple. It's the moment to tell him what Karin said, but I hear a distant laugh track. "Liv's watching TV again," I say instead, and Morten and I exchange a look, a momentary feeling of solidarity that drowns out the alarm bell about this new job. "I'll see if she's hungry." I tell myself that the moment to confront him about Karin denying knowledge of him is not while fish is broiling, nor is it during lunch. As I walk through the living room I have a flashback of sitting with Liv on boxes in our as yet hardly furnished house, looking through our newly developed wedding photos. She comes to the one of the horses in the field behind the church and looks up. "A horse walks into a bar," she says deliberately, trying hard to get it right, "and orders a drink. 'Hey,' says the bartender, 'why the long face?'"

I smile on my way up the stairs, then lean through the bedroom doorway. Liv's forehead is creased in concentration as she tries to follow the gibberish she is watching.

"Hungry?"

She turns her head reluctantly, but when she sees me her face lights up and she says, "Leo!"

"You remember me?" I say, stepping fulling into the doorway.

"I do," she says, so I take another couple of steps into the room, feeling my blood run warm inside my arms to my hands, and then she says, "From the couch."

I stop. "Oh."

"From looking at our wedding photos."

"But not our wedding."

She shakes her head, and looks back at the TV. She picks up the remote and turns it off.

"It's just nice to recognize you from the pictures," she says. "We looked so happy."

"We were happy. I think that was the best day of my life."

"You think?" she says.

"What?"

"You don't know?"

I try to read her face. The question sounds aggressive, but her expression is soft.

"I do know. It *was* the best day."

She smiles gently and gets up from the bed. "I tell you something, Leo." She walks to me. "When you know, you have to say you know. When I get my memory back I will say everything I know. If we only think, why say?"

"That's a good question."

"Will you also say what you know?"

"I will," I tell her, and the promise has the weight and shine of a marriage vow.

"Good," she says, and precedes me out of the room and down the stairs.

When we get to the kitchen, Morten looks like he's been sucking on a lemon. We have taken longer than he feels we should have. "I assume you like your fish well done," he says.

"I'm sure it's delicious," I say, pulling out a chair for my wife.

Morten says, "There is a moment, when broiling fish, when the oils in the meat are released under pressure from the fire. Some heat stimulates the oils, but more heat sends them streaming out all over the aluminum foil. That is their one moment too long under the flame. That is when the kitchen begins to smell." He sits. "I have had to open the window."

"Okay," I say, suppressing a smile, but Morten catches it anyway, and reddens with something like anger. I know he cares a lot about food, but I'm sure it's more than that. He looks peeved. He looks jealous. He has been left out.

We drive to the supermarket. Liv is in the front of the car with me, and Morten leans forward between our seats. We talk about the weather. Morten says it must be about the same temperature in Bergen. A few corners before the supermarket, Liv puts her hand on my thigh. Morten reaches between us to point out a tidy one-story house on the right and dislodges it.

"I move in there on Saturday," he says.

"Wow!" I say. "So close."

He just smiles.

"Is it furnished?"

"I suppose some people would call it that."

I keep my eyes on the road and do some reckoning. Once Morten has moved out, I tell myself, I'll both feel more comfortable and be able to find a way to get to the bottom of the situation. It's weird that he's chosen a place closer to us than to where he'll be working. Extremely weird. But if he disappeared completely, I might never know who he was. And my life would be so very quiet again.

The roads don't seem crowded, but the supermarket parking lot is, as are the aisles. I tear the shopping list in two and send Morten off on his own while Liv and I hunt around with the other half. She and I get separated nonetheless while I'm talking to the butcher. Not by much, about half an aisle or so, but enough for Morten to find her while my back is turned. When I locate her she's startled, staring at him open-mouthed with a box of tea in each hand. I go over to join them.

"How's it going?" I feign an investigation of the contents of Morten's competently stocked cart. He does work fast, there's no denying it. I've only got the turkey in mine.

"Leo," says Liv warmly, and embraces me as if we had been separated by mountains rather than jars of coffee. She tips her face up to look at mine, and she's beaming, perhaps with relief. What has Morten just said?

"Everything okay?" I ask her, and she nods and presses her cheek to my chest, but I don't believe her.

Morten says, "She doesn't remember making coffee."

Now I can't tell if I believe him. I just say, "Oh?"

Liv doesn't move.

"Look," Morten says. "She's holding boxes of tea. So I asked her if she doesn't make coffee anymore."

"She makes coffee."

"Not the way she used to."

"What way was that?"

"Right in the kettle. You put the coffee right in the kettle once the water has boiled, and then let it steep, and then pour it."

"Don't you get the grounds in the cup that way?"

"*Ja.* A little bit. But it's good."

"Norwegians don't use percolators?"

Liv pipes up. "We do."

"We do," Morten agrees. "But in the summer, outside? Coffee right in the kettle. You must come in the summer."

"I've been in the summer. We got married in the summer."

"You must come *camping* in the summer."

"The coffee you're describing sounds terrible."

"It's great. It's sort of . . . fruity. I know you'll like it. If Liv makes it. She made it so nicely."

Liv detaches herself from me and looks at the boxes of tea in her hands, and then puts them in our cart.

We continue.

"What time is Noriko coming tomorrow?" Morten asks back in the kitchen as we unpack the groceries.

"I invited her for three, so she'll be here at four."

"Noriko is a Japanese name," Liv tells us matter-of-factly.

"Sure enough," I respond, in that knee-jerk way we agree with the random declarations of very young, very old, and, I now know, amnesic people.

"Let me make the cranberry sauce," says Morten.

"Okay. Noriko will bring pies."

"Then we can do the vegetables on the day."

"What a team."

Liv drifts from the kitchen into the living room and sits back down with our wedding album. Morten phones for a pizza. I pull a lettuce and a cucumber out of the fridge and start to work on a salad. I make a trip upstairs to the bathroom. When I return, Morten has finished making the salad. I sit at the table.

It has taken me four days to learn how much better it

feels to lean back rather than forward when asking a loaded question. I do it now.

"How did you find out about the opening at the prep school?"

"Obituary."

"*What?*" I laugh, despite my resolve to be serious.

"Before I came, though. I picked up a Boston paper. They had the *Globe* in the library. And there it was in the classifieds. Apparently the guy had started the soccer program and had managed to make the team number one in the state for many years. Horribly difficult shoes to fill, but I called the school anyway. I was unhappy where I was, you see." He pours me a glass of wine. I can feel the smile on my face. I know he's going to tell a great story. "The wife of the owner of the team I was coaching was making me miserable. You know what misery is, Leo? Misery is a Norwegian man and an Italian woman. Guaranteed to drive each other insane. Plus she was the owner's wife. It's my policy, call me passé, never to touch a married woman. So I felt like a tiger in a cage, and there she was every other day, dangling raw meat just beyond the bars." With his accent, 'dangling' sounds like 'dankling', and I think it's a good word. He drinks, having finished assembling the salad. "At least that's how it appeared to me. She may have been doing nothing like that at all. I've been wrong before. Whatever was actually going on, a position at a prep school in New England looked like the perfect solution. I probably wouldn't have come for Liv's birthday if there hadn't been the possibility of a position, to tell you the truth."

He is challenging me to believe him. We stare at each other over our wine glasses. This is a sport I have no confidence in. If I pick up the gauntlet, what will I do with it? I let it go. We drink. After a while the pizza arrives.

I make sure Liv is asleep before I go to bed – to couch – myself. As I'm unfolding the blanket Morten says, "Sure you don't want to switch?"

Of course I want to switch.

"Nah," I say, "this is fine. We'd have to change the sheets and everything. This is fine."

"Okay," he says, "but I feel bad."

"Don't worry about it," I say.

"Slept down here before, have you?" he says, with the type of suggestive grin I never use, and hate in other men.

My hands go to my hips as the surge of irritation finally makes me say, "Karin says she doesn't know anyone at all named Morten."

The twinkle in his eye disappears. "You talked to her?"

"Of course I talked to her."

He purses his lips. "It's an extremely common name."

"Well —"

"So she's lying."

"Why would she lie?"

Now *his* hands go to his hips. He looks away from me and breathes out heavily through his nose. "She hates me," he says.

"Why?"

"Because she hates my father."

"That doesn't sound like Karin."

"No?" His eyes flash. "You know her so well? How often do you spend time with her?"

"Not often," I say, "but more often than you, I'd bet."

Suddenly Morten's face softens and he actually giggles. "Look at us!" he says. "Listen to us! We sound like teenage girls!" He drops his hands back down to his sides.

I smile, but only politely. It's true, what he just said, but so what? People bicker for a reason. They're frustrated. They feel disempowered. I've lost again.

"We can talk about this some more in the morning, *ja?*" he says, sounding conciliatory, possibly enhancing his Norwegian accent to remind me how foreign he is, to imply that we may merely have had a misunderstanding.

I'm tired. And afraid. I give up. "*Ja,*" I say, which makes him laugh. God damn me, I experience a flash of pleasure that he's found me funny.

NINE

I wake up in the dark to the sound of my name and a gentle tapping on my shoulder.

"Liv," I say. "Hi. Are you okay?"

"Yes, it's just, it's nine in the morning in my body."

"It's three o'clock?"

"Yes. Don't sit up. Stay there. May I sit?"

I shift myself so my back is pressed against the back of the couch, making space for her. She sits, and I wait to see what she will say. The heat from her body begins to connect with mine through the blanket and the sheet.

"I was thinking," she says. "Maybe I could lie down?"

"Of course," I say. But she doesn't lie down. She stands up. Maybe she can see the confusion on my face.

"Open the covers," she tells me.

In she climbs, and turns her back to my belly. I bring my thighs up against her bottom, but then I slide them away again.

"It's okay," she says. "Maybe put your body like you usually put your body?"

I slide my thighs back up. "Lift your head a little," I whisper, and when she does I put my arm under her neck and bend it across her chest. I lay my other arm across her waist. She says something I can't hear.

"What was that?"

She turns her face to the ceiling and repeats herself. "Maybe if we sleep like this I will remember."

If we sleep. Fat chance.

But we do. At least, I do. Spooning always settled me down.

I wake up to find Liv stroking the inside of my forearm. When she can tell that I'm awake she says, "You've always liked this, haven't you?" I can't see the expression on her face, but I can hear in her voice the excitement that she may have remembered something about me. I clear my throat. The combination of delight at the intimacy and miserable surprise at the question is a bitter glue.

I choose to be honest. "I don't think you've ever done it before."

"Well, somebody liked it," she insists. Then she realizes what she has just told me, and makes a horrified noise. She turns away from me and pulls the covers up over her head.

This is my one moment too long under the flame. I curl up behind her with my forehead pressed against the base of her neck and wait for the scorching moment to pass.

Karin calls on Thanksgiving morning. Morten is shaving. Liv and I are dressed and I'm making toast and coffee. Liv is quiet, standing at the sink looking out at the house next door. She's in my way but I don't move her. It feels like she wants to be near me.

"Will she talk to me today?" Karin immediately asks.

I hold the receiver out to Liv, eyebrows up. "Your mother," I tell her. Liv doesn't shake her head this time, but she doesn't reach out a hand.

"Don't be afraid," I say gently, trying not to plead. "She just wants to hear your voice. If you look like you are going to go crazy, I promise I will take the phone right back."

Liv steps over to take the receiver.

"Hello?" she says in English, uncertain, and then suddenly she is transformed. Hearing her mother's voice, Liv responds immediately with the sparkle and enthusiasm and lengthy run-on sentences of a child. The rest of the conversation is in Norwegian. I've never heard Liv speak so warmly to her mother, and I expect Karin is as surprised as I am. At one point Liv asks me if Morten is leaving on Saturday. I tell her he is, and she goes back to talking with her mother. The toast pops up but I leave it in the toaster.

When Liv hangs up she says Karin is going to visit.

"Great," I say. "When?"

"Sunday. The flight that gets here Sunday evening."

"That's wonderful."

Liv hugs herself. "*Vidunderlig.*"

"Honey," I say, and she blinks at me in surprise, but I don't stop to apologize for the endearment because I want to say something before Morten joins us. "Can you keep her visit a secret?"

"Yes. Why?"

"I just . . . I can't understand Morten's relationship with your family, and I don't want him to know she's coming before he needs to."

She blinks some more.

"Does that make any sense to you?"

"No."

"Can you do me this favor?"

"Okay."

I exhale, realizing I've been breathing very shallowly for I don't know how long. I push the toast back down into the toaster to warm it up again. Liv watches me.

"Do you trust me?" I ask.

"I do," she says. "I search but I can find no reason not to."

We smile at each other.

"And we have matching wedding rings," she says. We hold up our left hands and look at them. I wonder, if Liv doesn't retrieve her memory, could she fall in love with me again? And if she falls in love with me again, will it be a second chance to tell her about my boys as if I haven't been keeping them a secret? I drop my hand when I hear Morten's heavy footfalls on the stairs. Liv keeps looking at hers.

"I smell toast," Morten announces when he enters the kitchen, reminding me to pop the toaster. He goes to the fridge and takes out a fat salami I don't remember him buying, and the wheel of meals begins to turn again.

"Time to put the bird in?" asks Morten when Liv and I are looking at more photo albums in the late morning.

I look at my watch. "Is that the time? Wow, thanks for staying on top of things, Morten." I start to get up but Morten holds out a hand.

"I've got this," he says, and goes back into the kitchen without waiting to see if I protest.

I look at Liv to see if she wants to be involved in getting the turkey in the oven, and she's yawning hugely. Her eyes stay closed for a while when her face relaxes again, so I guide her upstairs and tuck her in bed for a nap like a toddler, an invalid, a woman near the end of her life rather than in her prime. Sitting there on the edge of the bed, I can't help thinking of the end of my mother's life. I recognize the panic of abandonment in the painful banging of my heart.

I go down the hall to the study to call Noriko at the hospital. When they have paged and located her, the first thing she says into the phone is, "I can't wait."

"Great," I say, and then, "I don't know how much more of this I can take."

"Tell me," says Noriko, and I can hear her friendly, steel-reinforced professionalism asserting itself.

"Liv is completely erratic. Every day is different. Every *moment* is different. She must have imagined that getting her memory back would be an obvious process. I guess I did, too. But one thing's not leading to another."

"I'm going to make an appointment for her with the psychiatrist," she says firmly.

"It's the right thing to do, isn't it?"

"Don't be an idiot."

"Thanks."

"Can I change when I get there?"

"Where?"

"There. Your house. Thanksgiving dinner."

"Right! Of course."

"Also, is he handsome?" On cue, Morten steps out the back door and starts collecting leaves and pinecones, and I scrutinize him from the study window.

"I don't know. Probably."

"Try harder."

"Well, I'd guess maybe seven out of ten women would say so."

"Then I won't be late."

I'm washing lettuce when Noriko rushes into view, huffing and puffing up the driveway, white stockings sticking out under a heavy black coat, bright red dress in a dry-cleaning bag slung over her shoulder. "Morten!" I shout, and he joins me at the door to greet her.

I take a pie box from her and pull her up the last step and into the warm kitchen. I hug her, and then I say, "Morten, Noriko. Noriko, Morten."

Morten kisses her hand.

"Hold off, sweetheart," Noriko says. "My manicure isn't until next week."

Liv arrives in the kitchen doorway, and we all smile at her as she squints in the light.

"What's happening?" she asks, not recognizing Noriko at all.

"Thanksgiving," I tell her.

"Oh! Oh no! I've got to change," she squeals, and runs back the way she came.

"Oh dear," Noriko says, and Morten and I nod in agreement.

I test the gravy while Noriko goes to the hall bathroom to transform herself. When she emerges, Morten sweeps her into the living room to dance. I wonder if the action is spur of the moment, or if he's been planning it since Noriko arrived. He is, of course, a very good partner, if a little too precise. The old Liv would have called him a little too Norwegian in his movements. From my vantage point in the doorway I see the beginning of Liv coming down the stairs. I can tell from the hem of her skirt that she has put on her wedding dress –

her mother's ivory wool, hand-embroidered, traditional Norwegian costume. I've got two left feet, but still I cross the room and lead her from her trance on the bottom step into the dance.

At the table, we toast the turkey, we toast Noriko's dress and Liv's, we toast our extremely strange reunion. Once we have started eating, Noriko leads the conversation, as I had hoped she would. She asks me what the theme of my students' photo show at the college will be next year.

"I'm considering making it a study in local contrasts," I tell her.

"Such as?"

"Well," I begin, but Morten interrupts. "Such as Noriko and Liv?" We laugh, in our different ways, and Noriko turns to him.

"And what would you choose as your theme for a photo show, Morten?" She's leaning her elbow on the table, chin on her palm.

"Nurses, of course!" Of course.

Liv is staring at Morten. He has also noticed this. I scrutinize him for discomfort, but he gives her his big, ready-for-anything smile. I'm afraid she's just going to keep on staring, and even Noriko stops chewing, but suddenly Liv seems to wake up and says, "Delicious," filling her fork and delivering it to her mouth.

"How about you, Noriko?" I ask.

"Well, I'd do color. You know me. Maybe a collage of photos of sequins. Something with texture. Crazy photo patchworks of sequins. Something like that." She does a sweep of her wine glass which lands at her lips.

"I would do northern Norway," announces Liv, and then keeps eating.

"Tromsø," Morten says.

Liv shakes her head. "No, no. Behind the mountains. In the valleys. Maybe just one valley."

"You've been there?" Morten asks, his ice-blue eyes unblinking.

Liv looks up from her food. "*Ja da.*" I know this phrase. She means of course she has and we should know that.

Morten asks her when and her eyebrows twitch and draw in. "I went . . ." She looks down and to the left, scraping around in her brain, retrieving no further information.

"How would you do it?" I prompt.

When she finally looks up at me she says, "I don't know anything about photography."

"Sure you do."

"Oh. Did I?"

"Sure. But that doesn't matter. Just tell us about some of the aspects of the north you would try to get across in the photos."

She thinks for a long moment, and when she speaks it is as if she is blind to us. "I would make the photos huge. Black and white. Cold. Dark rocks hiding in the snow. The northern lights but not with color. Just the shape, which is like ghosts. I would fit them into the walls, like windows. The light in the room would have to be a cold light as well . . . but you'd get the feeling that somehow you are protected. You are inside, and the ice and snow, the powerful shapes of the Arctic Circle are on the other side of a wall. But you don't feel completely safe. The landscape will always be there, every time you look out the window." She looks down at her food but not as if she sees it, and I can feel the rest of us wondering whether to speak, but then she looks up again. "And not only that. You will always find it fascinating. Something tells you to stay inside. Something else tells you to lose yourself in the negative of the landscape. The Arctic is guaranteed not to be green. Like death." A pause. "It is the only dream I have right now. That I remember. Every morning I wake up from death." Tears she seems unaware of roll out onto her cheeks as she focuses on us – first on Morten, then Noriko, then me.

To me she says, "Isn't there a specialist I can go to?"

I look at Noriko.

"Monday morning at nine-fifteen," she says.

TEN

In the morning, Morten says he's going out to buy a few things for the house he'll be renting. Liv wants to see more of her life, so we drive the route she usually took when walking to her office, one of the two commercial spaces in a converted house near a funeral home. I slow down as we approach and Liv looks all around us, clearly unaware that her office is just to our left. "That one," I finally tell her, and she leans over me to see through my window. No response. "Nothing? Want to go inside?"

"Of course," she says. She's in a good mood, energetic, unworried. Maybe knowing that her mother is coming has made her feel like her trials will soon be over. Karin will set the record straight. I wish I were as unconcerned by what it might actually be.

Fortunately I know the code that lets us through the door. Inside her office – one large former-bedroom with its own bathroom – the air is very cold and still. I stand just inside the door, but Liv charges on in, going straight to her desk, looking through her notebooks and her address book, shaking her head and tutting at her inability to remember anything. She doesn't seem so much frustrated as amazed. She's not afraid of who she was. She turns a little green vase around and around in her hands.

"Where did I get this?" she asks me.

I have to admit I don't know.

She nods, uncritical, and sets it back down.

"What does this phone do?" she says in front of her office machinery.

"That's not a phone, that's a fax machine."

"A what?"

I walk over to stand by her side.

"Fax. Facsimile. No?"

"Definitely not."

"You didn't have one in Norway?"

"What does it do?"

"It sends documents, via the phone line."

She studies it. "You dictate?"

"No, you put the document in here and as it moves through, the machine somehow transmits the words to a printer in the machine you send it to."

"Wow," she says, "America is very advanced."

"I guess. Yeah. It is. But I'm pretty sure they're using similar machines in Norway too these days. I think maybe you just don't remember how they developed. You had an older one first, a really clunky one, and you bought this new one when it stopped working."

She keeps looking around the office, but being told she's lost enough years to be bewildered by technological development has taken some of the stuffing out of her. She pulls open a drawer in the bank of four second-hand file cabinets on the opposite wall, and is surprised to see stock rather than files inside. "Buttons," she says.

"Yes. You sell a lot of buttons."

"What else?" She closes that drawer and opens the one below.

"I think it's actually mostly buttons and Christmas ornaments, but also candlesticks, and some salad servers."

"Like ours?" she asks, and her use of the word 'ours' warms me in a way my coat can't seem to. I can't help but grin. When I don't say anything she looks back at me. "Yes," I tell her. "Like ours."

I think she'll smile, but she has confused herself. She shuts the drawer and returns her hands to her sides, where they hang.

"Enough?" I ask.

She nods at the floor. Rain suddenly whacks against the window above the desk. We should probably stay for a while, but Liv so palpably wants to be at home that I say, "We'll make a run for it."

I blast the heat in the car and think hard as I drive, chewing my lower lip, keeping my eyes on the wetter and wetter road. Liv gazes out the window.

"How would you like to go to Norway?" I ask.

"Okay," she says.

"After your mother comes. If her visit doesn't help."

"Okay," she says once more, and we don't talk again until we've run from the car to our house and I'm hurriedly unlocking the door.

"It's dark in Norway at the end of November," she says.

"That'll be interesting," I say as we step through into the house. "I've never been in the winter."

"Yes you have," she says, surprised, as we de-coat.

"When?"

She thinks, suddenly unsure of herself as we stand close together inside the door, waiting to get over this hump before moving into the kitchen. "Well, don't you remember skating?"

"Liv, we've never been skating."

"But . . ."

"We've never been to Norway in the winter." I'm starting down a steep hill. "Who are you thinking of?" I take her hands. "Who is Morten?" She lifts her shoulders like a child who doesn't know what she's in trouble for.

Footsteps scrape the back steps. Through the storm door we can see a hooded Morten grinning at us between an umbrella and a bouquet of celery leaves and spring onions. Then there is a sickening squeal of brakes, a muted thud of contact, and we watch a black and white dog spinning across the slick road, coming into contact with the curb, bobbing its head and yelping in pain. Morten looks on for a moment, and then looks back at us, still smiling. By this time I've grabbed my coat again and am pushing past him down the steps. Liv follows me and when we reach the dog we hear a woman shouting as she approaches from a house across the street, "Oh God! Oh God!" Liv has the dog's head in her hands. It wants to look at the running woman but it yelps when it tries to turn around. "I didn't know the door was still open!" she says. "Jackie Jackie Jackie are you okay?" The woman tears her coat off so we can help her get the dog onto it, the pitiful cocker spaniel always looking at its owner for reassurance in its pain, and then we carry it across the road and into her car. Liv and I stay with the dog inside the cold car while the woman goes inside to call the veterinary hospital and tells them she's coming.

"How could someone hit a dog and drive away?" Liv asks as she strokes the shivering dog's head.

"How could someone watch and have no reaction?" I ask.

Seated in the living room holding coffee mugs, Morten and I watch Liv go upstairs for a rest.

"You didn't want to get involved with the dog?" I say.

He looks at me in surprise. "You needed me?"

"No, but —"

"You didn't need me. That was obvious."

I should say "That was obvious once I'd left the house, but not before," but I shrug. Have it your way.

He gets defensive. "Why should three people worry? No, four people. Why should four people worry if three is enough? *Two* would probably have been enough."

"That's very . . . practical."

He seems to take this as a compliment. "Yes. Also, I was holding things."

And smiling.

I hear the TV go on. I say, "The vet agreed to see the dog right away, but we have to wait all weekend for the psychiatrist."

Morten nods, looks into his mug, then out the window. "I wonder if that's too soon, or not soon enough."

"There isn't anything I don't wonder about anymore."

Morten smiles faintly and looks over. "What will you do? Your vacation is over, isn't it?"

"I might go in and ask for a substitute, and then take off till January."

"Can you afford to?"

"If my insurance covers this kind of thing. I have to dig out my policy."

"I don't start work until January. Let me help. I can talk to her more about the past. See if I can ring some bells."

"That's what I'm worried about, Morten."

"What?"

"I'm worried about the bells you might ring."

He stares at me in surprise for a moment. "I'm the bogey man, am I?"

"Somebody is."

"Why not you?"

"Because I was thousands of miles away from her when she lost her memory."

"So was I."

"So you say."

"What? I was in Atlanta! Coaching the —"

"Yeah, yeah, I know. So you said. Going crazy over the owner's wife."

"It's true."

"Prove it."

My heart is pounding, not because I'm afraid of fighting but because I'm *prepared* to fight. But the conversation stops there. Morten doesn't say another word. He stands up from his chair, stares down at me for a long moment, and then turns his back. I hear him set his mug in the sink before he puts on his coat and leaves the house.

He may feel he's drawn a line in the sand by walking out, but I *know* I did. For once I made a demand. Maybe he's right to be offended that I did, but I don't mind. I'm proud of myself, and twenty minutes later I know I'm right to be when the phone rings and it's Morten.

"Can I come back?" he says.

"That depends."

"I'm not angry. I'm sorry. Everything must be difficult for you. Too many questions."

"Yeah. Thanks."

"I was driving around, and I calmed down, and I saw a skating rink."

"The Ice Arena."

"Yes. Why don't we go skating?"

We do.

Noriko joins us. I make Morten call her himself, which he does with grace, and I imagine her hopping around in excitement on the other end of the line. I pour hot tea into a thermos but Morten stops me from screwing on the lid until he has poured in a large splash of rum and spooned in a lot of sugar. "I'll drive," he says, putting on a brightly colored wool hat and going out to warm up the car. I'm left looking at the thermos, shaking my head in wonder.

"What a great idea," I say to myself as I climb the stairs to get Liv out of bed. "What a fucking great idea."

"What?" she asks.

"Morten is like a living subscription to *Gourmet* magazine."

"Why?"

I grab a sweater for her. "Because he put rum in the tea."

She giggles. "Where's mine?"

I lift her from the bed into a hug she doesn't reject. "First skating, then rummy tea."

She pulls back excitedly and points to the television. She's been watching figure skaters compete. I turn it off.

"This outfit isn't nearly pretty enough," she tells me.

"It's fine for rehearsals," I tell her as we leave the room.

It has stopped raining. Noriko is standing on the sidewalk in front of her house like a child waiting for the school bus. Liv and I are in the back seat. As Noriko approaches, Liv's hand strays to my knee and she looks up at me.

"Noriko," I pronounce slowly and quietly.

The skating rink is windowless but brightly lit under the blue-black sky. The parking lot surrounds it like a moat. Deep woods darken its far side. The only sound outside is the crunch of our feet on the ground and the occasional swish of a passing car.

Inside, the black rubber floor silences our feet but the air wobbles with sound. The organist in her raised box in the far corner calls for a doubles skate and starts to pump out "Never Can Say Goodbye". Noriko owns skates so she sits right down on a bleacher and starts lacing up. Morten gets ahead of Liv and me in the rental line and requests a pair for himself, then Liv and I belly up to the skate bar and place our orders. "Shoe size?" asks the geezer in a t-shirt behind the counter, and Liv says "Thirty-six," which means nothing to him so I lift one of her feet to look for a number on the sole, and tell him it's six.

By the time we're ready, Noriko and Morten are already skating. He has taken her right hand in his, and has his left on her left hip. He catches sight of us standing at the edge of the ice, and directs Noriko toward us. As they swing by he shouts, "Jump on in, the water's warm!" Noriko looks like she has seen the Promised Land.

"He's fun, isn't he?" says Liv, just as I am about to step forward and give her a hand onto the ice. I stop and watch his antics for a moment.

"He's really fun," I admit.

We move from the rubber onto the ice and steady ourselves before gauging the flow of traffic and choosing our moment to join in.

"Is he married?"

"No. You are, though."

She looks up at me in surprise, unbalancing us both. My heart plunges. I think she's forgotten again. But no, she's just frustrated with me. "I know *that*." We push off again. "I'm just worried about Noriko. She loves him so much." Noriko and Morten are doing the barrel, where you face your partner, hold both hands, and spin.

"Head over heels," I agree, and I feel her find her balance. Liv's a pretty good skater. I'm not, and she stays with me.

"I think I am young to be married," Liv says.

I concentrate on my unstable feet. "You weren't at the time," I tell her. "But maybe you are now."

Suddenly Morten stops in front of us in a spray of ice. "It's time to change partners," he announces, man enough to pull off the drip at the end of his nose. "Noriko is throwing off my sense of superiority. I need some time with a beginner." His eyes flash and I imagine him spiriting Liv away under the bleachers like the villain in a silent movie. For a moment Noriko tries not to look as disappointed as I am, but we enjoy being together, so we shrug and begin to lift our hands toward each other. Morten slips between us with an instructive arm around my waist and makes off with me, shouting, "Glide, Leo, glide! You skate like a drunk!"

ELEVEN

To move into the furnished house he's renting, Morten only has to repack his clothes and toiletries bag and put them back in the car before driving over.

"What about your stuff from Atlanta?" I ask him as he sets his bag down by the back door.

"Yeah," he says, "I'll have to see about that. There's not much. I've got some of it in the car."

The trunk of the BMW doesn't look very big. He distracts me from the thought by saying, "I'll have to buy some more sweaters."

I walk him out to the car, coatless, and stand with my hands in my pockets as he slides his bag onto the back seat. Door closed again, we stand looking at each other. He laughs, misinterpreting the look on my face. "I'm just moving down the road, Leo," he says, wrapping his arms around me, which is awkward for me but clearly natural to him. Before I know whether to lift my arms to put them around him he slaps my back and goes.

I stand in the warming kitchen, listening to the quiet,

wondering what Morten's departure will mean for Liv and me, and also thinking about coffee and toast. My stomach rumbles audibly, but before I get breakfast going I jog lightly up the stairs to the guest room, looking around for signs of Morten having spent six nights in our home, but there aren't any.

Liv appears in the kitchen when I'm halfway through my second piece of toast. Her toes point in like a little girl's, her flannel nightgown sticks to her long socks.

"Hi!" I say. "Breakfast?"

She scratches her messy hair. "What am I supposed to be doing?"

"What do you mean 'supposed to'?"

"I look at you moving around the house, and there's something telling you what to do. When you finish something, you know what to do next. I don't even know what day it is."

"Don't be fooled. I'm improvising. It's morning. Breakfast just seems appropriate."

"I think I need to look at the clock more," she says.

I go to where she's standing and put an arm around her to bring her to the kitchen table. "You'll remember. You'll find a routine that suits you," I tell her. And myself.

Seated at the table, she perseveres with her questions. "You've got energy, though. What is *moving* you?"

"You are."

Liv looks surprised. I go to the fridge.

"I want to know what I would be doing if I were the old me," she says.

I pull out the orange juice, and as Liv waits I see an opportunity for fun and games – an opportunity the old me would have had trouble taking. Liv doesn't remember the old me, so anything goes. Glide, Leo. Glide.

"Let me think," I tell her in mock seriousness as I pour a small glass of juice and then begin to pace the kitchen like a professor. "Usually you are so exhausted from all the Disney movies you watched the night before – not to mention the jumping on the bed, the hide-and-seek, and the pin the tail on the donkey – that you sleep in until at least, oh, seven-thirty. Then you jump out of bed, and you slam the bathroom door behind you and come out again, in, um, thirty-five seconds, looking perfect and smelling like a powder puff." She laughs. I clear my throat. "You give me a passionate kiss, leaving me with half your lipstick, and then you rush down the stairs to prepare breakfast in bed for me." I check her expression; she looks happy for me to go on. "You . . . Uh . . . You whip up some French toast and a fragrant fruit compote, put a little aquavit in my freshly ground, freshly perked coffee, and carry the tray back up to our room. All this has given me time to brush my teeth and put the red rose from your dressing table between them. You put the tray on my bedside table. Then you give me another passionate kiss."

"With the rose still between your teeth?"

Oops. "Oh yes. In fact, sometimes you refuse to kiss me if I don't have a rose between my teeth."

"I see. Is that all?"

I make her wait a beat or two. "No."

"Oh." We blink at each other, then she says, "The old me is maybe being motivated by *you*."

"Well," I say, suddenly timid again. "I guess there's no accounting for tastes." I turn to put the kettle on, and she gets up from the table. Her little white hands creep around me in a hug from behind. "What would you like for breakfast?" I ask, heart banging again.

"French toast," she says into my sweater.

. . .

"I don't know who you are," I say to Liv as we enter the bedroom.

"Neither do I," she says.

"I don't know who I am anymore either," I tell her, and reach for her waist.

"Neither do I," she says, and puts her hands on my face.

"I feel like I'm seventeen. My palms are all sweaty."

"I *am*," she begins, and then stops herself from saying "I *am* seventeen," which makes me take my hands off her body, but she keeps hers on my face. I feel the pressure of her pinkies hooking in at the back of my jaw to keep me from pulling back, and when she stands on her tiptoes to kiss me her lips feels like Liv's lips, thirty-one-year-old Liv's lips, and I slide my arms around her again.

Our lovemaking feels like a first kiss. Not the shocking, sloppy kind that grates against your teeth. The ideal kind. Liv mews and giggles and shudders, and comments on the goosebumps that flash across my buttocks when I come. Afterwards, with me still inside her, she looks up at me from our hug, rubbing her still-socked feet against my shins. "That felt like a first time," she says.

"It did," I agree.

After more hugging Liv suddenly flinches.

"What is it?" I ask her.

"I might get pregnant," she says.

"You won't," I assure her. "You have an IUD."

"What is that?"

I feel myself retracting, in danger of slipping out of her. I grab tissues for us both from the box on the bedside table and we disengage and take turns in the bathroom. With the old

Liv I might have remained naked, might have gotten back into bed, but I dress for the IUD conversation. So does she.

"An IUD is a little thing you can have put inside you to stop conceiving," I tell her.

"I have one of these?"

"Yes. Sometimes it's called a coil?"

"Oh. Yes. I know this thing. *Faen!* What else is in me I don't know about?"

I think. "That should be it. Although, wait, maybe some fillings in your teeth."

"Okay. That I am not surprised about."

I smile.

"I think I will look at the wedding again," she says, and goes downstairs.

I stay upstairs to tidy the bed, and replay the moment where she said, "That felt like a first time." Her beautiful face, less worried for a moment. Less distant. But then, pulling the bedspread back up over the pillows, I replay the moment when she almost said, "I *am* seventeen." So she feels she's seventeen, but she knows what a first time is like. How many first times does a person have before they can confidently say they know what to expect from a first time? She's told me about the crushes of her high school years. She's told me her first sexual experience was in her first year of university.

I shake my head to try and clear it, and replay the view of her face looking up at me, the warmth in her eyes. We have matching wedding rings. She's looking at our wedding album. She wants to remember me. She hasn't spent a second trying to remember Morten. She wants to remember *me*.

· · ·

We go for a walk around the Titicut reservation area, bake an apple pie, repeat ourselves repeatedly, nap to manage the stress. In the early evening, when Noriko calls, Liv's watching TV. I'm in the kitchen staring at our pie.

"I have to talk, Leo," she says after my hello. "Can I talk?"

"Can you ever."

"I'm serious."

"Okay. Of course. Talk away."

"I just spent the afternoon with Morten."

"Where?"

"We went for a walk out at Freetown. Now I'm wondering how I'm going to sleep tonight with this electric current buzzing in my blood."

"Yipes."

"I know."

"Did he touch you?"

"He squeezed my hand at the door as he left."

"And that was enough to get you going?"

"That was plenty."

"Sounds like it's been a while."

"You know it has."

"So is it that, or is it him?"

"I think it's him. I mean, I meet men all the time."

"Course you do . . . Well, I can understand the attraction."

"You can?"

"Sure."

"Excellent."

"But do you trust him?"

Noriko considers the question. "Clearly I trust him enough to walk alone with him in the woods."

"Uh-huh."

"But my heart?"

"Yeah. How about your heart?"

"I don't know. A few warning flags, but I don't think I care. I can't help it."

"He's kind of magnetic. What I don't understand is why Liv doesn't seem to be affected by him one way or the other."

"She's not responding to us the way she did before either."

"True. True. I wonder if she ever will again."

"If she doesn't, is that necessarily bad?"

Neither of us answers the question.

TWELVE

That night, Liv and I share the bed. I let her take the lead on sex, and she doesn't initiate again. When we get downstairs in the morning, there is Morten, quietly squeezing the juice from a dozen oranges. I realize he hasn't returned the house key I lent him. A prickle of irritated sweat blooms under my turtleneck. Knocking on our door during the day is fine, but letting himself in is something else. Liv stops next to me in the doorway.

"Will you make the coffee?" Morten asks me, and then immediately asks Liv how she is, ignoring the fact that we haven't moved from where we are standing. I want to ask him whose house he thinks he's in, taking over breakfast and asking me to do things, but I can't because I've never refused to partner with him on meal-preparation before. Liv says, "Okay," and I start moving again. I go to the stove and fill the kettle. Liv sits at the table.

Morten says his place won't feel like a home until after Christmas, after there has been something to celebrate there. "Your home is a homey home," he says, and then asks what our plans are for the day. I tell him we're probably going to clean the house.

"No updates from the hospital?"

"Updates? Like, 'Oh, sorry, we've suddenly realized we *did* see a brain tumor'?"

"Of course it's not a brain tumor," he scoffs.

"Why 'of course'?"

"Because," he says, and then stops squeezing the oranges for a moment's thought. Changing tack? I can't tell. "Because she would be having terrible headaches if she had a tumor, wouldn't she?"

"Spoken like a true soccer coach."

Liv says, "Please be nice, everybody."

We eat. I say nice things about the juice. Then Liv gets up from the table, smiles distractedly at us both, and starts to put on her coat and one of the hats she has knitted for me.

"Where are you going, Liv?" I ask gently. It's as if she's sleep-walking, and I don't want to startle her.

"Leaves," she says, and closes the door behind her. Morten and I go to the window over the sink and watch her begin to collect leaves in the yard. After a while she straightens up and looks around, first at our house and then at old Alice Fulsom's next door. She obviously has no idea which is hers. She starts for Alice's, so I go to the kitchen door. Outside on the step I see that Alice has appeared as well, a rare and interesting occasion. As I start across the lawn I see Alice gesturing, and can practically feel her huge saggy arms swinging under her old tan cardigan. Liv turns and sees me, appears to thank Alice, and comes my way.

"Are you awake?" I ask as we meet in the driveway.

Liv thinks. "What a terrible question," she says. "I don't

know the answer." She brushes past me to go back inside. At the top of the steps she says, "Please don't ask it again."

I ask Morten for the house key before he leaves.

"Oh?" he says when I do, out of earshot of Liv.

"Yeah," I say, putting my hands in my pockets, "I've got a friend coming from tonight."

"A friend?" he says. He hasn't reached into his own pocket yet.

I make myself smile. "Yep," I say. "From out of town."

"Not great timing, is it?" he says, tapping his front pockets to see which one the key's in.

"I don't know. Could be good."

"Okay then." He holds the key out to me, as if he's just granted permission.

"We'll call you, okay?"

"Just come by," he says, opening the back door. "I don't have phone service yet."

Liv leans forward in her hard airport chair, straining to see, as though a huge crowd were pushing through the doors toward us when only a few people are dribbling out at a time. I take a few deep breaths to calm myself, and then I ask Liv if she's nervous.

"I don't think I have the right words," she answers, very matter-of-factly, without taking her eyes off the doors.

"It's the right thing to do, isn't it?" I keep watching the doors, too, hoping that Karin won't arrive before I feel better.

Liv finally looks over. "I think so. What I remember about her is good."

It's hard for me to characterize Liv's relationship with her mother. In all photos, they look very sweet together, and when Karin has visited us – twice in the past four years – her stay has been pleasant and uneventful. Sometimes, though, when we've all been in the kitchen or living room together, when Karin's been talking to me, I've caught glimpses of Liv looking at her with something like disdain. Her eyelids come down a little; her normally soft regard hardens. It happened on both visits. I can't remember what Karin was talking about when Liv looked at her like that. I think I imagined at the time that Liv might have been feeling a bit puritanical. That was all I could come up with.

The energy changes in the waiting area as a noisy trio of men in suits and overcoats pushes through the exit, and a steady stream of other travelers follows. It's all black and navy coats for a moment, and then Karin stands out in a red wrap. I see Liv's eyes open wide with recognition. We both stand up, and Liv runs to her. I approach more slowly and watch as the two women embrace, and as Karin lets Liv run her fingers along the lines around her eyes.

On the way home, Liv tells Karin, "It's not just the events I want to remember. It's the street names, and dates, and other important numbers. Each day is a little boat, and I have no compass."

I feel I know a little of what Liv means. Liv's memory was my memory. She was my phonebook. She remembered birthdays. She remembered the name of the plumber.

Karin begins to recite a verse from the back seat: "'There are lots and lots of people who are always asking things, like

dates and pounds-and-ounces and the names of funny kings .
. .'"

She pauses in case we want to chime in, but we don't so she continues, half-singing. It's almost a lonely ballad. "'And the answer's either sixpence or a hundred inches long, and I know they'll think me silly if I get the answer wrong.'"

"Why do you know that poem?" I ask her, when Liv doesn't say anything.

"I don't know," she says, and I look at her in the rear-view mirror, catching her eye, questioning her.

"I honestly don't know," she insists, and I look back at the road. When I glance at the mirror again she's staring out the window, shaking her head. "I'm getting old."

Liv turns in her seat and stares at her.

At home I lug Karin's baggage through the living room as mother and daughter sit on the couch together, and Karin points and says, "You can leave that blue one down here, Leo. It's full of photo albums."

I put her other suitcase in the guest room, use the bathroom, then choose a towel to put on the end of her bed. When I get back downstairs, Liv is lying with her head in her mother's lap, and Karin is singing to her. Her voice is as clear as a bell in the upper register, a little husky down low, like her speaking voice. I walk through to the kitchen and fill the kettle. When it boils I make a pot of tea and put it on a tray with mugs and milk and the box of marzipan Karin has brought, and bring everything to the living room. Liv appears to have fallen asleep. Karin is stroking her hair.

"She obviously hasn't forgotten her childhood," Karin says as I pour. "Whenever I had time, I sang her to sleep."

"Her memory disappears in high school," I say. "Do you have any idea why?"

Karin looks down. Her lips are unmistakably pursed. After a moment she says, "There are a lot of things that I would rather she didn't remember."

"Oh?"

"Don't you feel the same way, Leo?"

"Of course. But I don't think the memory of them will shatter her. I mean, we're here to help, right?" We watch Liv breathe a few breaths. I say, "I want to know who Morten really is."

"Are you sure?"

"Most of the time. I wish I had a photo of him to show you and get it over with, but I haven't taken any."

"I know who he is, Leo," she says quietly, still looking down at her daughter.

My heart goes cold. I'm not completely surprised, though. I'm just . . . scared.

"Who is he?"

Now she looks up at me. Her eyes aren't light blue like Liv's. They're gray.

"Liv never told you about him. That is what she wanted. So I cannot."

I can't help raising my voice. "But now she's—"

Liv's eyes flutter open and she sits up, blinking at us, stretching her arms up above her head, smiling, saying something I recognize in Norwegian. "Good morning," I reply, grinding my emotional gears to produce a genuine smile. "Actually, it's much later than our usual dinner time."

In the end I just bring a bunch of cut-up carrots and celery and some cheese and crackers into the living room and we look at photo albums. Liv sits between Karin and me. Just before we open the first one, Karin says "Wait!" and jumps up. She pulls a cassette out of one of the pockets of her shoulder bag and works out how to use our hi-fi equipment. I recognize the music as one of her earliest recordings. Unmistakably Karin, unmistakably younger. We settle back together on the couch, and Liv opens up a large white album. Her baby album. She turns the pages.

Liv and Karin head up to bed right after we finish all the food on the table, and as I wash the dishes I feel myself becoming furious with frustration that Karin's arrival hasn't illuminated anything. I decide I have no choice but to try again with Morten. I'll get the truth out of him if I have to stay at his all night. I dry my hands, throw the towel at the table, grab my coat and stomp out to the car. I drive too fast and squeal to a halt in front of Morten's house, getting out of the car before I lose my resolve.

When he opens the door he is delighted to see me and wraps a piece of silver tinsel around my neck, pulling me through the door and into the living room. Noriko is on her knees at the base of a Christmas tree whose top scratches the ceiling and whose branches are heavy with bulbs of frosted glass. Damn. I hadn't stopped to consider that she might be there. Her elation scotches any thoughts I had of a showdown with Morten. He pries my right fist open, considering with interest the force required, and presses a mug of mulled wine into my hand.

I improvise, noting to myself how much easier it's getting with practice. I tell them I needed a night out, and saw the lights in the window. Noriko expresses a little concern that Liv has been left alone in bed, as if I had abandoned a toddler to the night, but I remind her how deeply she sleeps lately.

"Plus," says Morten, "you've got a friend staying, right?"

"That's right," I say, going over to the couch and sitting down to hide my discomfort. Although the tinsel irritates my neck I leave it there, and smile at them. "It's a bit early for a tree, no?"

Noriko looks adoringly over at Morten. "He insisted," she says, and starts decorating the tree again from a new box of silver bulbs. Morten smiles sheepishly. As I listen to them chatter about the unpredictable old man who owns the Christmas tree farm, I feel relieved that I haven't been able to call Morten a liar tonight. I shake my head at myself internally as I realize I wouldn't have had a leg to stand on without telling him about Karin, and it isn't time for that yet. I sit back, and when they say something funny I go ahead and laugh.

THIRTEEN

A curly-haired woman wearing fall colors and a chunky necklace is bending over behind a desk, pulling out all the drawers. I'm guessing late fifties. This is Dr. Shapiro ("Call me Ruth or I'll scream"), the psychiatrist. It's Monday.

She finds her note pad and comes back around to join Liv and me in a semicircle of small, upholstered armchairs. Liv wanted Karin to be present as well, but Ruth drew the line at one family-member. Even that was unusual, she told us. It surprised us all that Liv chose to keep me with her. "He's the one I don't remember," she said simply, as if the reasoning should have been obvious to us. Karin left, reluctantly, smiling from the cheeks down, worried from the eyes up, clutching Ruth's directions to a coffee shop.

"Oof!" Ruth now says as she sits, and when she meets our eyes she laughs. "I know. 'How can this woman possibly help me locate my memory?'"

We laugh nervously along.

"I've been on vacation. When your specialty is trauma and dissociation, you take vacations whenever you can."

"You've dealt with amnesia before, then?" I ask.

"Of course. I've also had it."

"What happened?" asks Liv.

The doctor's merry face grows a little serious. "Make you a deal," she says. "I'll tell you what happened to me if you tell me what happened to you."

"Okay," says Liv. "I'll try."

The emotional contract concluded, Ruth looks down at her pad and then up at me. "I think it's very important that you are here, Leo," she says. "Today, at least. Liv wants you here. This doesn't mean that I've ruled out a role for you in her situation, though. I have to consider everything, like the police. All lines of enquiry. Liv's an adult, and she's here for her memories. At this point, she is happy to have you with her, but there may come a time when she isn't. Or I'm not. Will you be able to accept that?"

I nod right away, without trying to imagine what it will feel like to be kept out of their sessions. I'm encouraged by the firm hand she's taking. I feel she'll be nice to Liv, and that she'll keep me in my place.

"Also," she continues, "I won't be talking to you, just to Liv. Okay?"

I say okay.

"Okay with you, Liv?" Ruth asks.

"I guess so. What if he has questions?"

"He waits."

Liv looks at me. "You can wait?"

"Sure," I say.

Ruth returns her intelligent eyes to Liv. "Memory retrieval can be overwhelming. If your amnesia is in fact the result of psychological trauma you need to understand that digging for it can also be traumatic. I want to know how you would like to approach the situation, since your memory will then be your responsibility. Although we'll of course develop a plan for managing any difficult memories once we have them to work with."

Liv licks her lips. "It doesn't sound like I can just put up a few signs because my naughty dog has run away and expect that you will bring him back."

Ruth smiles and considers this. "Nice analogy. Well, let's see. By coming here you have begun to put up the signs, and we may be able to find your naughty dog. But he might bite."

Liv takes time to think. "Could I suddenly remember things that I had blocked out even before this happened?

"It's possible. It's more likely to reveal what your brain is choosing to hide from you now."

We wait for Liv to speak again.

"I'm interested," she says quietly.

"And not frightened?"

Liv shrugs lightly.

"I don't get the feeling that you understand that we may uncover terrifying memories," Ruth says.

Liv thinks again. "I feel like I must be a very happy person. My childhood was so wonderful, and my mother. She would have taken care of me. What could have happened?"

"The worst things you can imagine, Liv."

"Like what?

When Ruth responds she pauses between each item on the list, giving Liv time to think, watching for any reaction. "Like witnessing a murder. Like *committing* murder. Like sexual abuse. Like rape."

Liv says, "None of these things happened to me."

"They might have."

"They didn't."

"Liv," Ruth says firmly, "they might have."

"*Now* you are frightening me."

Ruth nods gravely. "We need to make sure that you are as ready as possible for your memories."

"Well," Liv says, tugging the sleeves of her sweater down over her wrists. "I'm here. We are doing this."

Ruth brightens. "Okay, let's tinker with a few nuts and bolts. We have lots of wonderful memories to uncover as well, no doubt. For example, Liv, do you remember Leo at all?"

Liv beams me a smile, and then looks back at the doctor. "Not yet," she says confidently.

Ruth laughs. "But you like him."

"I like him *so* much," says my Livvie.

"And where were you born?"

"Bergen."

"Oh yeah? Nice?"

Liv smiles broadly. "Very nice!"

"What did your father do for a living?"

"I don't know." She thinks. "My mother was a folk singer."

"And where was your father?"

"I don't know."

Ruth looks at me. I nod.

"Do you know your father?"

"No," Liv says sadly.

I nod again.

"Where did you go to school?"

"Bjørndalsskogen *skole*."

"Was that elementary school?"

"Yes."

"How about high school?"

"Ortun *skole*."

"And college? Did you go to college?"

"No," she says confidently. She sees Ruth look at me. She turns to look at me too and asks, "Have *you* been to college?"

"Yes."

Liv doesn't take her eyes off me as she thinks. Then she says, "Should I have gone to college?"

I look at Ruth, and she nods at me to go ahead and speak.

"You *have* been to college," I tell Liv.

"In Norway?"

I shake my head. "Here."

Liv turns back to Ruth.

"No recollection?" Ruth asks.

After a moment's effort Liv says, "Nothing."

"Okay," Ruth says, betraying no concern. "Now then, does the name George Bush mean anything to you?"

"No."

"John F. Kennedy?"

"Yes."

"Who is he?"

"Dead president."

"Marilyn Monroe."

"Yes."

"Tom Hanks?"

"No."

"Mother Teresa?"

"Yes."

"The Rolling Stones?"

"Of course!"

"Great. Excellent. Did you remember your neighborhood when you saw it again?"

"Which neighborhood?"

"Here, where you live."

Liv shakes her head.

Ruth writes, stops writing, and sits back. "Can you tell me a little about yourself?"

Liv nods. "Yes. I'm from Bergen."

"Uh-huh. Got that. Great. How old are you?"

Liv looks at me, I guess because I'm the one who told her how old she was on her birthday. I smile at her. It's all I can think of to do. She turns back to Ruth. "I'm thirty-one."

"How old do you feel?"

Liv's eyes dart toward the window. She doesn't answer.

Ruth says, "Never mind, Liv. Never mind. What was your house in Bergen like?"

Liv smiles. "We had a big, creaky apartment."

"Who did?"

"My mother and I."

"No siblings?"

Liv shakes her head. The doctor shoots me a look. She's been briefed about Morten. If Liv and Morten really played together as children, Liv would be able to remember, but as she didn't find out they were siblings till later, then this answer makes sense. I shrug. Ruth makes a note.

"Is Bergen a good place to be a child?"

"It is if you have my mother."

"Tell me."

"She is so creative!" I've never heard Liv talk about her mother this enthusiastically. "She is a singer. Very popular. Always friendly, always energetic."

"About her profession?"

"About everything. But mostly about me."

"That's nice."

"Yes. Sometimes not. But I remember, when I was maybe eight she bought me a great big, hairy, white dog, Ivan, and wherever she sang, at an outdoor festival or a coffee shop, didn't matter, she insisted that Ivan and I be allowed to come along." Liv smiles into the middle distance at the memory. "In the summer we traveled to the folk festivals around the country."

Ruth stays quiet, giving Liv the space for more memories.

"That is where I started loving crafts. I love Norwegian crafts," Liv says. "A button is never just a button."

"What is it, then?"

"Jewelry."

"Ah. It makes perfect sense that you chose your particular profession then."

Liv is brought up short. She closes her eyes. "Oh, yes," she says, having dragged herself over the gap in her memory.

"According to Leo, you're the most successful distributor of Norwegian pewter on the East Coast."

"Wow," Liv says. "I'm awesome." And then she laughs. "Unless I'm the *only* distributor of Norwegian pewter on the East Coast."

Ruth laughs out loud, and she and I exchange a look. She's impressed; I'm proud.

Ruth says, "We've jumped ahead. My fault. Let's go back again. So, you remember the name of your high school. Let's see how much you remember of your*self* at school."

Liv nods, but doesn't say anything right away.

"Were you sporty?"

Liv laughs and shakes her head.

"When I was in high school," Ruth offers, "I had a whole wall of my room reserved for photos I had cut out of magazines. I spent a huge amount of time folding tiny pieces of tape for sticking up these pictures. Did you do anything like that?"

Liv smiles at Ruth's memory, and then thinks. She folds her arms, scrunches her eyes, tips her head to the ceiling, exhales. We wait. Her head comes back down, but her eyes are still closed, and she starts to shake her head.

"No?" says Ruth. "Well, how about —"

"I had an autograph book," interrupts Liv.

"Did you?"

"It was yellow, with tiny blue stars on the cover. My mother gave it to me, and when I opened it she had put her own signature on the first page."

"Do you remember who else signed it?"

"The next time I went to hear my mother sing I took it upstairs to the guy who controlled the spotlight. I had a crush on him. For a long time. I didn't know the other guy singing that night, but I asked him for his autograph too. I remember he told me I made his day. Um . . . I had my English teacher sign it, because I knew she was writing a book. Maybe it would be a best seller. And then, of course, I had all my friends sign it, and I asked them to write under their names what they wanted to be famous for."

"Was this a birthday gift?"

"I think so."

"Do you remember which one?"

Liv shakes her head. "Sorry."

Ruth makes a note. "Not to worry," she says. "Do you think this autograph book still exists?"

"I'm not sure. Why?"

"I'd be interested to see how many of the signatures are male, how many female," Ruth says.

"Oh?" says Liv.

Ruth twinkles. "I'm sure both Leo and I want to know how many boyfriends you had."

"I'm not sure I was interested in anyone but the man behind the spotlight."

Ruth writes, then asks, "How old was he, do you remember?"

"I never asked him. I think I didn't want to know."

Ruth clearly wants to know. She does a good job of keeping her eyebrows gently lifted when she's talking with Liv, displaying openness, lack of judgment, but they come down when she takes a note about this spotlight man.

"How about your mother? Who did she have eyes for back then?"

"Sorry?"

"You say she was very friendly."

"She is."

"What do you remember about the men in her life?"

Liv thinks. "I remember two from my childhood. Pål, and then Arthur. I think they were both drummers." She laughs. So far the memory doesn't seem troubling. "And they were crazy about my mother. That was the problem. I think they were both a little younger than she was. Too young, I guess. They weren't ready for the whole package."

"What was the whole package?"

"Her, me, Ivan."

"So what happened?"

"They would keep trying to take her away for weekends and trips abroad, and she would keep showing up with me next to her. Eventually they went away."

"Were they nice to you, though?"

"Oh yes. Especially at the beginning. Lots of stuffed animals, sweeties, that kind of thing."

"You must have been pretty small, then."

"They liked to think I was."

"What about when you were in high school?"

Liv thinks again.

"Nothing?" asks Ruth.

"Nothing yet."

"That's okay. Let's talk about winter in Norway. Christmas. Tell me you don't eat reindeer."

Liv giggles. "We don't. But we ride them to church in the morning."

Ruth laughs, and carries on with her friendly, strategic questioning.

"What do girls buy for men in Norway?"

I note the use of 'men' rather than 'boys'.

"Do you remember ever shopping for a tie?" Ruth continues.

Liv shakes her head. "I always knit them socks."

"Who?"

"Blue for Pål. Red for Arthur. In Norway, it is considered bad luck for a woman to knit something for a man she isn't married to. Probably because when Norwegians knit it's so complicated. But there is no superstition about girls knitting for their mothers' boyfriends."

"Do you still knit?"

Liv looks at me for help and I gesture at the beautiful sweater I am wearing – white snowflakes against a black background, and an intricate red motif around the yoke. "Christmas eighty-nine," I say.

"After you were married," says Ruth.

"Of course," says Liv.

"I'm assuming you've only been married once," says Ruth.

"So am I," Liv says.

So am I.

"Can you remember your first kiss?"

"With Leo?"

"No, I mean your first kiss ever."

Liv smiles, but then looks confused. "I wish I could," she jokes weakly. And then she puts her palms over her eyes. We wait. "I'm so tired," she says.

Ruth nods sympathetically. Very sympathetically. I'm impressed by how long she remains silent. Eventually she looks at her watch, but only to note the time. Finally, she says, "Stop there?"

Liv nods, still with her face on her hands. After a moment, I stand up. Ruth continues to observe Liv. Liv takes a deep breath and then puts her hands on the edge of her seat, as if to push herself up to stand, but still she just looks at the floor.

I pull Liv's coat off the back of her chair.

"Can I ask a question now?" I ask.

Ruth stands up. "Certainly."

"Are we getting anywhere?"

"This sudden exhaustion could be a sign." She reaches down for Liv, who allows Ruth to lift her to her feet. "I'm going to let Leo take you home now, to let your brain behave how it wants to," she tells her, "but there may come a time when I won't."

FOURTEEN

On Tuesday I have to teach. I was able to avoid Monday's departmental meetings, but today no substitutes are available for my class and I have to go in. I don't feel like the department has tried very hard to find one. I did let slip that Liv's mother had arrived, so they probably feel I've lost my excuse for staying away.

Karin says I can leave Liv with her, but I'm too nervous about Morten dropping by unannounced. Karin says she'd be perfectly happy for him to come by so she can deal with him, but I'd never get any answers that way. I tell her that if she gets rid of Morten and Liv hasn't had a say in it, we might both be in big trouble. I remind her that we need to be ready for Liv to remember *everything*, and that she'll pass judgement on how we've managed what is going on. Karin stares into my eyes, unblinking, unseeing, thinking things through, then promises to stay out of sight upstairs, and not to answer the phone or the door.

It's a great feeling, having Liv along on my commute to the college. How many people bring their spouses to work for a day, or even an hour? Suddenly I can't believe it's not normal.

Liv doesn't want to sit with the students and takes a chair against the back wall of the room I share with painting classes. I love the sharp odors the oil paintings exhale, the dusty auras of the watercolors. If I had been born before cameras I would have had to be a painter.

When the students come in – nine of them – Liv smiles and says hi to the ones who acknowledge her. I don't say anything about who she is. I thought I would. I imagined introducing her, and the students turning around in their chairs to take her in more fully. "My muse," I thought I might tell them, but now I feel in danger of showing off. I want to impress her. I want her to know me and love me, but not think I'm an idiot. So I try not to showboat and just get down to business.

It's a class on post-sunset photography, taking advantage of available light, experimenting with shutter speed, the pros and cons of light trails, tripods. I prefer the class on darkroom techniques. That one feels more artistic, and there's something about experimenting with developing that almost always encourages students to start experimenting with shooting. I get to show a lot of my own photographs in this class, though, so I'm glad it's this one Liv has come to.

She doesn't take her eyes off me. It reminds me of the one time a female student briefly became infatuated with me, except that this time the attention is more than welcome. Now and then I turn off the lights to project examples of photos onto a screen. I had to take a lot of color shots expressly for this class, but I show black-and-white ones as well. Each time I turn the lights back on I look at Liv, and she's smiling as she blinks in the light, or tipping her head thoughtfully to the side, until about ten minutes before the end of the class, when I show a black-and-white photo of a sculpture from Frogner Park, taken at the end of our six-day honeymoon drive along the crinkled Norwegian coast from Bergen to Oslo.

We arrived in Oslo at nearly ten p.m., checked into our hotel, and put together a picnic supper from the remainders of our trip supplies — bread, cheese, tomatoes, cider. We were walking-distance from the park, and ended up having our dinner on the steps of the extraordinary display of Gustav Vigeland's larger-than-life granite sculptures of naked people at all stages of life — playing, loving, brooding, fighting, mourning, commiserating, dying — arranged around a central column of stacked bodies.

"Amazing!" I exclaimed as I opened our ciders. Liv started slicing the cheese on a paper plate.

"Almost too much," she said.

"I know. It might be hard to digest our food next to all this energy."

"It might be hard to chew, even."

I laughed and cupped her cheek, and we drank to us. I also lifted my bottle in salute to the statue we were right next to, a huge young mother on all fours playing horsey with a pair of mischief-faced children, a boy and a girl. The children have wound their mother's long braid around her head for a rein and she holds it between her lips. The children are larking, but there's no sense of precariousness for them. Their mother is broad and peaceful, dependable, beautiful. The sun began gently to release its hold on the day as we ate in contented silence. What can you say in such a place? I looked around at the other statues near us. I'd never seen anything like them. When I turned back to Liv, she was perfectly framed in the space under the mother's belly. Normally you have to get your camera out very quickly at sunset because the light can change in a few seconds, but not in Norway in June. I put down my bread and picked up my camera, adjusted the settings, and took a series of shots. The one I like best, and which I now show my students, is the first one I took. The top of the photo cuts the children off at the ankle, showing their feet, the mother's undercarriage, and space. Liv's silhouetted profile is looking up, her pointed nose guiding your eye to the mother's pendulous breasts. I show the class another one as well, of the whole statue, to illustrate what happens to the dark-light balance when you zoom out, and then I turn the lights back on, telling myself not to expect Liv to have remembered our honeymoon.

She's not looking at me this time, and her face is so pale it's light blue.

"Liv?" I say, and she turns her head my way, leans forward, and vomits violently onto the paint-spattered floor.

I run between the desks but stop short of where I want to get to because the vomit has traveled so far. She had raisin-heavy muesli for breakfast, and coffee, and it is now spread way out from the toes of her ankle boots. I pick my way around to her side and rub her back. She's shaking. I look up at the class. Two of the girls have approached, and some of the guys have stood up too.

"Go get the janitor, please," I say to the one closest to the door, and he goes. "Class is obviously over," I tell the rest.

"Can we help?" asks one of the girls, then suddenly Liv looks up at me.

"We did that," she says. Her eyes are round with terror.

"We went there, yes," I tell her. I rub her back some more, and she looks at the floor again.

I look at the helpful girls and tell them, "I think I better take care of this myself. But thanks. You all go ahead. We'll be fine. We'll wait for the janitor."

They shuffle out, murmuring. The story will spread. That must not matter now. I shut them out of my mind.

Liv whispers something, and I crouch down to hear her. The smell near the floor makes me want to gag. I say, "What's that, honey?"

"We did that," she whispers.

"Yes. After the wedding."

"No. No, Leo. No. No." She looks at me, her face now wet with tears and snot. "Leo. Leo." Her breath catches in her throat. "His name is Kjell." She pronounces it 'Hyell'.

Her eyes beg me to figure out what she's telling me.

"Morten, you mean?"

She nods, and lets out one sob, wrapping her arms tightly around herself.

"And you went to that park?"

She shakes her head rapidly and points to the now empty screen. "We did that."

"You did what?"

"I had very long hair."

I think. "You played horsey, as children?"

She doubles over, forehead on knees. It seems like she's trying to stop herself from keening. Then she turns her face to me. "We weren't children," she whispers.

This sinks in. I whisper back, "So, it wasn't horsey?"

I hear the wheels of a mop bucket.

"Puke?" the deaf old janitor shouts from the doorway.

I move Liv to another chair while the janitor sloshes his mop around, and I pack up my projector and lock it in the supply closet. I get both our coats and ask Liv if she thinks she can walk. She nods.

"Thanks a lot," I call to the janitor as we reach the door.

"Yeah, well," he says.

As we pass the men's bathroom I tell Liv to wait just a second while I go inside to get some wet paper towel for her boots.

"Toilet paper too," she says. When I come back out she leans against the wall and lets me kneel at her feet to clean them up while she blows her nose and wipes her face dry. Once I've thrown the paper away I help her on with her coat and get into mine. "We'll talk at home," I tell her. "Let's get home."

Back in our kitchen, I help Liv out of her coat and she moves weakly through to the living room.

"Want to change out of your jeans?" I ask her and she looks down at herself. "Let's go upstairs and get you some fresh clothes," I say.

"I need to brush my teeth," she says.

"Whatever you want," I say. Karin comes into the living room. "We'll be back down in a moment," I tell her, but she says, "I'm coming," so we all go upstairs and into the bathroom.

Liv takes off her jeans and hands them to me before stepping over to the sink and putting toothpaste on her toothbrush. She looks at herself in the mirror and her eyes ask the eyes in the mirror a question. No answer. She brushes. I dump the jeans in the corner next to the laundry basket and leave the room to get her some other pants. I pull some pajama bottoms out of her drawer and hurry back to the bathroom. Liv is spitting and rinsing out her mouth. She puts her toothbrush very carefully back into the glass, and doesn't look in the mirror again before turning around to face her mother and me.

"Here," I say, holding out the pajama bottoms, but she doesn't reach for them right away. She stands there in her light blue turtleneck sweater and her red underwear and her purple socks and says, "I don't want to talk to either of you right now. I want to talk to Ruth."

Her *voice*. She's thirty-one again.

I say, "Okay," and Karin says, "But—" and Liv holds up her hand.

"Okay," Karin says.

Liv takes the pajama bottoms and puts them on. Then she shuts herself in the bedroom.

"Come on," I say to Karin, although I want to stand with my ear to the door as much as she does. I make her go down the stairs in front of me. Karin marches all the way through to the kitchen and then turns to face me with her feet planted and her arms folded across her chest.

"What happened?" she demands.

"Kjell," I say.

She flinches. "She told you?"

"She told me this name. She told me Morten is Kjell."

"What else?"

"Not a lot."

"Tell me."

I don't want to. I ask, "They were lovers?"

She doesn't say anything, just grinds her teeth.

"Actually," I go on, "I don't need to ask that. I know."

She drops her arms.

"That's all I know, though, and it looks like that's all I'm going to get out of Liv for now. But how about out of you?"

"I want to tell you, Leo."

"Tell me."

"We must wait."

"I can't tell if you're being loyal to Liv or protecting yourself, Karin."

She spreads her hands. Her eyes look sad, and conflicted, and scared.

I soften my tone. "Just one question. Please."

"Okay," she says, "but maybe I won't answer."

I nod. "When Liv and Morten, no, Kjell, were children, did you arrange to have him come to your apartment and play?"

"No! Of course not, I did not do that. Who said that?"

"He said that."

"No, I did not."

"When *did* they meet, then?"

"This is question number two." Suddenly she looks sincerely apologetic, and comes to where I'm standing. She takes my head in her hands and leans her forehead against mine. She smells of cinnamon and leather. "We wait."

We wait. We have coffee. Eventually we go back upstairs. The bedroom door is now open. Liv has closed the curtains and gone back to bed.

I go to the study and try Noriko at home.

"Hello?"

"Noriko, Morten isn't his real name."

"Why not?"

"Because he's been lying to us."

"Why would he lie about his name?"

"To help him lie about everything."

Silence.

"What *is* his name?" she asks.

"Kjell."

Silence.

"I can't even imagine how to spell that."

"K-J-E-L-L."

Silence.

"He's been lying about everything?"

"Okay, maybe not everything. He is Norwegian. He has known Liv before. I don't think he's her brother, though."

"So what is he?"

"They were lovers, in high school."

Silence, then Noriko's voice takes on a defensive tone.

"This is maybe more of a problem for you than for me, Leo."

I don't know this Noriko. I try to reach the one I remember as my friend and confidante. "If you were here, you'd understand why it feels evil to me."

"When will you be sure if it is or it isn't?"

"No idea. Karin isn't telling me the whole story in order to protect Liv's privacy."

"Okay, well—"

"Noriko. *Nori*. When Liv remembered him she threw up all over the floor of my classroom."

When Noriko speaks again, her voice is more recognizable.

"Have you called Dr. Shapiro?"

"Liv has. I don't know what they said, though."

"Do you want me to come over?"

"Liv's asleep. I'll call you."

"I'll be by the phone."

Right after I hang up the phone it rings.

"Leo!" Morten's voice says, "I've been trying your number on and off for an hour or something. I've got a phone now!"

"Kjell," I say, my mouth completely dry.

Silence, then I hear him clear his throat. Then silence.

"You were lovers," I say.

I listen to him breathe.

"She has remembered," he says.

"She has remembered something."

"What has she said?"

"I'm not going to tell you that. I want you to stay away."

"I can help."

"I don't want your help right now. Karin is here to help."

Silence again. I don't know what else to say, so I just hang up. I stare at the phone. It rings. I pick up the receiver, but I don't say anything.

Kjell says, "Are you sorry that I came?"

"Yes."

"Are you sorry on absolutely all counts that I came?"

I hang up again.

Liv is hungry when she gets up and Karin makes her a sandwich. Liv tells us she has an appointment with Ruth at five, and she wants us both to come with her, even if we can't come in.

Driving over I look in my rear-view mirror, signaling to make a left turn, and there's just enough light left in the afternoon for me to see Kjell driving behind me. Maybe my nervous brain is playing tricks on me. I don't say anything to the women, and make a turn I hadn't planned on, without signaling, and then another. I feel like I've lost him, or maybe it wasn't him. I decide it wasn't him. When we arrive at the clinic and start walking through the parking lot, though, he gets out of his car in a space closer to the building. Karin's ice-cold hand grips my wrist, then she recovers herself and begins to talk brightly to Liv, distracting her, pointing at something across the street, picking up the walking pace.

I hang back. I'd rather duck straight into the building with the women, but I have to do this. It's either now or when we come back out. I know he won't go away if I avoid him. His eyes dart around as I approach. I sense, or I hope I sense, a thinning of his comfortable veneer.

He's standing by his car door. I stand next to the front bumper and fold my arms. "What are you doing here?" I demand.

"I want to help."

"By doing what? Lying? Telling fairy tales about Liv and her family? Seducing Noriko? This is helping?"

He ignores this and says, "Let me help Liv remember."

"No."

"But I love her," he says.

I grab fistfuls of my own hair. "I'm her husband, for God's sake! How can you talk to me like this?"

"She loves me too!"

"Remembering you made her *vomit*, Morten. Kjell. *Jesus*. You're a liar. Keep your distance."

I stride away and get to the clinic door. I'm almost through it, I'm closing it behind me, when he grasps it with both hands.

"You have secrets too, Leo!" he hisses, and my stomach plummets. I leave him holding the door.

Upstairs, Karin is leaning her back against the wall opposite Ruth's office.

"Ruth doesn't want us in there," she tells me.

We go back downstairs, and I stop inside the glass door to look for Kjell's car. No sign of it. We walk back out into the now very dark afternoon, and Karin stops me, her face a picture of despair. "It doesn't feel like she's here anymore. I am with her, but she isn't with me."

"Well . . ." I'm about to say that for a while Liv is going to be wherever her memory has taken her, but suddenly cool Karin is crying, sobbing on my shoulder. I'm holding her up and she's shouting next to my ear, "What are they saying up there, Leo? What is Liv telling that woman?"

I'm suddenly so irritated want to shake her. I had been depending on her to keep calm. A few people walk by on the sidewalk. Thanks to them I wait out Karin's panic. When she finally steps back she's wide-eyed, like a frightened horse. I really want to be able to go with the flow, but this isn't a flow, it's a flood.

"Say something, Leo. Please."

"I can't answer your questions," I tell her. "And you won't talk. I'm in the dark. So it looks like we're stuck with silence."

Karin is right to be worried. The ride home is so tense I never feel the warmth from the heater, and when we get into the house Liv stabs her coat viciously onto a coat hook and stands in the middle of the kitchen waiting for us to get our own coats off. Her hands are balled into fists on her hips. Karin and I turn like two naughty children to face her fury.

"You made him go away and you didn't tell me why," she says to Karin.

"How can you blame me?" Karin says, and switches to Norwegian. Liv responds in Norwegian. They raise their voices, they both say "Kjell". Neither of them ever looks at me. I move away and stand by the kitchen table. I'm not in trouble, clearly, but I feel threatened. None of what they're saying has anything to do with me, I'm sure, and I wonder as I observe them, straining for any shred of understanding, if it ever will again. Liv looks like she's lost weight overnight. Her pale skin is stretched tight over her cheekbones. Their fight is huge, and foreign, and looks like it should be taking place outside in swirling snow rather than in a Bridgewater kitchen.

A point comes when Karin appears to be desperately asking a question that pulls Liv up short. Karin asks again, and Liv runs from the room. We hear her pounding up the stairs. Karin turns her back to me and goes to the sink, looking out the window. After a moment I say, "You're not going to tell me anything, are you?"

She shakes her head, so I go upstairs.

Liv is also looking out the window, in our bedroom. She doesn't turn around when I stop in the doorway, although she must have heard me, so I cross the room and stand next to her, looking out as well. I don't dare interrupt her thoughts. We're there a long time. I look at Alice Fulsom's house. I try to figure out which room Alice is in, but I don't see light at the edges of any of the blinds. My heart rate starts to slow down as I accept that the wait could be very, very long.

It *is* long. I'm surprised Liv hasn't said anything yet. The fact that she hasn't moved away makes me think she will speak, though, so I stay. For a while I wonder if I should ask her a question to see if that unfreezes her, but decide that just being present, available for when she is ready to talk, sends a better message.

I start thinking I should rake Alice's yard again. She got out and did it herself two years ago, wheezing around at the end of her rake, but I didn't see her outside once the following fall. Her house is the same size and shape as ours, and long ago it may have been a similar shade of white. The green paint on the trim is cracked and curling. The wood underneath looks thin and insufficient. I went over last year to ask if she'd like me to clean up the leaves for her, and knocked on the storm door. No answer. I opened it and knocked on the inner door, and then tried to turn the ancient bell in the middle of it, but it was rusted and useless. Maybe she was in a distant room. Maybe she didn't hear well. Maybe both. I tried the handle and the door shuddered open.

I had imagined that the house would smell stale with decay and old air, but even so, the first noseful was a shock. "Alice?" I called from the dark entry hall. "Alice? It's Leo, from next door." The heavy ticking of a large clock tempted me on into the kitchen. The brown linoleum on the floor was worn thin after years of Alice's slippered comings and goings. The kitchen can't have changed since she arrived, save maybe for the portable electric burner on top of the original wood-burning stove. There was an oval table and two chairs, and a large, sagging wingback chair in the corner by the cold black fireplace. In front of the fireplace was a small wooden cradle, clearly hand-made, with an ancient teddy inside, the only evidence of family in the room. Maybe her father made it for her. Maybe she made it for her own daughter to play with, now gone. This one poignant piece of evidence was almost worse than none at all.

I retraced my steps and crossed back to my own house –

warm, bright, smelling lightly of the scented candles on the windowsill. I pulled on some gloves, tucked a few garbage bags into my pockets, then went back out and raked Alice's yard.

"I know why I married you," says Liv suddenly, returning me to the present, to the bedroom.

I turn slowly to look at her, too scared to feel delighted.

"You never expected me to adapt to your mood swings."

"I don't really have mood swings," I say.

"It's so nice."

"I'm upset now, though, Liv."

She nods sadly and then takes my hand, interlacing our fingers.

"He says he loves you," I tell the window, and her little hand squeezes mine. "He also says you love him."

I wait for her hand to say something and it goes slack.

"Liv?" I say in a voice that tells her I need her to speak.

"I did."

I inhale deeply, exhale loudly, forcing myself not to let her hand go.

"We were going to have a baby."

"Oh . . . In high school?"

"Yes. My mother was against it, and wanted me to get an abortion, tried to force me, but I wouldn't go. I was so happy, but then Kjell disappeared, poof, gone completely, and then," she rattles out the story as if to get it over with, "I miscarried and the baby was gone too. Everything gone, and my trust in my mother gone also, because all my life she agrees with me and supports me and suddenly she is shouting at me, not listening."

I unlace my fingers and take her in my arms. "You could

have told me this, Liv. We fought about children because you didn't tell me this. We didn't have to."

She shakes her head against my shirt. "I left Norway to change my life. I did not bring it here."

I'm so sad. So, so sad. "I could have—"

"Maybe if we had had one more fight I would have told you."

"One more fight?"

She looks up into my face.

"You remember our fight?" I ask her.

"*Ja.*" She looks back down and says "I'm so sorry" into my chest.

I stroke her head. After a while I say, "Karin is in pain downstairs."

Liv pushes away from me, her face screwed up in disgust.

"Karin's in pain? *Karin's* in pain?" she almost shouts, and then she's aghast. "Oh, God, Leo," she says. "I have been so terrible to you."

"No, honey, no." I reach out to her but she puts up a hand and scrambles onto the bed.

"You don't know what I've done," she says.

"Yes, I do."

"You don't!"

"So *tell* me."

She grabs the bedspread and bites it between her teeth, squeezing her eyes tight shut.

"You played sexual horsey with Kjell. You got pregnant. You loved him. I know these things now, Liv. It's okay."

Eyes still closed, teeth bared in their grasp of the bedspread, she shakes her head.

"A couple of days ago you promised you'd say everything when you got your memory back," I remind her, and then I stand and wait. At some point, she will open her mouth. The question I have to ask is pounding in my head. *What happened in Oslo?* To ask would be like kicking her, though. I bite the inside of my cheek. Half a minute later she opens her eyes, sees I'm still there, and lifts all the bedding to burrow inside. She says something.

"What's that?" I ask, bent over where her head is.

"I need Ruth," she says, louder.

She has another appointment in the morning. I put one hand on her shoulder, one hand on her hip. "Yes," I say, and then, "I'll bring food up later."

I have no idea how to talk to Karin, so I go to the study and end up staring at the phone for a long time. Then I realize that I can find out the number of the last caller. The last caller was Kjell. I think to go to the window to see if he is sitting in his car somewhere nearby; he must have been, earlier, in order to follow us to Ruth's office. I don't see it, at least not through the glass. I heave the window up and lean out to look farther down the street both ways. No car. I close the window again and return to the phone. I dial the number for last-caller ID, and write down the last number to call our line. My heart is pounding. If I call and he answers, I'll . . . what? I've already asked him to stay away, and at least so far he is staying away. I have a confusing feeling of fascination. What is he doing? What is he thinking? Is he experiencing fear? Triumph? Shame? I wonder if he has flown away. I hope he has. I hope he hasn't.

I pick up the receiver and dial. When he answers I ask him, "Do you really have a job at Chapel Hill-Chauncy Hall?"

"No," he says.

I hang up like I've been burned. I stare at the phone for just one second, imagining him staring at his, willing me to call him again. I leave the room so I won't. I go downstairs and put on my coat and rake our reclusive neighbor's yard in the dark until my shoulders scream.

FIFTEEN

I have a dream. I am walking along an icy road lined with houses that huddle and sag and look medieval. It is evening. The surroundings are unfamiliar, but I know that I am on my way home. At first I'm alone under the iron-gray sky, and then little by little people begin to emerge like walking gargoyles from the shadows of doorways and alleys. They are hideous, sloppily dressed in heavy clothes, covered in gritty dust. Their features are huge, their strides uneven. They are not directly threatening, but their unhappiness is oppressive. As I turn a cobbled corner I realize that one has separated himself from the crowd and is walking silently by my side. He is different from the others – strong, upright – and he carries a decorated Christmas tree on his shoulder. There is no doubt that we are heading for the same place, and that place is near.

Before we get there I sweat through whether or not to let him in when we arrive, but when we are in sight of the door and a window's welcoming light I know that I have to get there first, but also that I have to open the door for him and let him precede me into the warmth.

Liv is inside. She turns to us from her position by the fire, wearing what my imagination has established to be the normal, highly embroidered Norwegian costume of the Middle Ages. She looks somberly from the gargoyle to me and from me to the gargoyle. He props the Christmas tree in the corner and when he stands up straight again I see that his stony head is elaborately carved into hair that exactly resembles mine. Liv asks the gargoyle, "Who's your friend?"

The shock of the question wakes me up.

The morning is colder, and dark, a sickroom with the shades partly drawn. Karin knows that she needs to occupy herself, so I draw her a map and she walks to Liv's office to see what she can do that needs doing. I need to occupy myself as well, so I take my camera along when I drive Liv to see Ruth. These days have thrown me way off balance, and I feel a bit more like myself with my camera bag slung over my shoulder. I wait with Liv until Ruth calls her in, and then I leave the clinic on foot, purposefully, trying not to think about Liv and her secret life. A light snow has begun to swirl like it's only joking about falling. I take a full turn around the parking lot, on the lookout for Kjell's car, and then set out to find subjects to photograph and force time to pass. Time is like a fishing line I'm trying to haul in. Anglers get excited about what might be on the hook, but that's not how I feel. I tell myself to look around.

The wires crisscrossing the center of town are flashing with Christmas lights. Some people are shopping. Their coats are dark and a few of their shopping bags are red. Not so good in black and white. I find myself heading down to the alley behind the drug store, the hairdresser, and the hardware store. In the open dumpster are hair spray canisters (how long since those hairstyles collapsed?), an empty box from a delivery of painkillers (how long since those aches returned?), a broken answering machine (how many messages were missed?) and bags and bags of discarded packaging (how many of those new products are now in the dump?). I finish a roll and settle another one into the camera. Back on the street the Christmas lights look like the flashing monitors in a hospital room. The gloom is getting to me, but I decide to embrace it — something I can do more easily when I have my camera along. I go back to the car and drive south. Over by the junior high I see a clutch of cross-country runners heading out. They wear gloves and hats, but their naked white legs flash against the black trees. Woods line the road. I'm approaching the skating rink. Before I get there I turn down the driveway to the dump. I park by the recycling stations, change to a zoom lens, and head for the trash. The air is too cold for the mound in the pit to stink too badly. The snow, wetter now, has begun to obscure some of the names on the bags and boxes and to smooth out ragged edges and dented sides. This is the moment I'll try to capture. All through this trash are things people have forgotten or want to forget. Here and there, no doubt, are things people have thrown out by mistake and are racking their memories to find. Until the snow covers the dump entirely I can photograph the disappearance of things.

Back in the car outside the clinic, Liv shoots out her hand to stop me from turning the engine on.

"Kjell is here in Bridgewater," she says.

"Yes."

"Take me to see him, please."

"Now?"

"Yes, please."

"Why?"

"I just . . ."

She can't finish the sentence.

"What does Ruth think?"

Liv bunches her hands into fists and presses them into her lap. "I won't lie to you, Leo. Ruth does not think I should go."

"Then—"

"She thinks he should wait for his place in line."

"That sounds like good advice to me."

"Who gets to decide where that place is, Leo?" she demands fiercely. "I do! *I* do!"

"I don't think—"

"Who knows best, Leo? Nobody. We just need to deal with this issue, and Kjell is this issue, so we deal with him. Please take me."

I exhale through my nose at the windshield.

"I've seen where his house is, Leo. I remember driving past it." She rubs my arm to make this sound less of a threat, more of a simple fact. "I can remember how to get to his house. So unless you keep me prisoner in our house, I'm going to get there."

I think the prisoner idea is a good one, but I start the car.

"What am I going to say?" she keeps asking on the way over. I should have gone back into the clinic and talked to Ruth. I'm Liv's husband, and I'm driving her to see her ex-lover. I'm throwing myself naked into brambles. But I love her. I'm a nice man. I ask, "What do you *want* to say?"

She shouts without warning. "'Where the fuck did you go, you bastard? You bastard! You fuck fuck fucking BASTARD!"

I've never heard Liv use this kind of language and it's hard to keep my eyes on the road. For a moment I wonder if I should pull over and let her calm down, but then it occurs to me that maybe it's actually time for someone to start yelling at Kjell. I haven't been able to, but maybe Liv will go through with it.

I pull over against the curb in front of his house. There's a light on in the living room, but his car isn't there. The weather has turned really cold, so maybe he's closing it up in the one-car garage. Liv has undone her seatbelt and gotten out before I've turned off the car. I hurry to catch up, and I join her at the front door. My mouth drains of saliva and I want to run but Liv is already knocking. No one comes to the door. Liv tries the handle. The door is unlocked. Liv walks in, small and furious and brave, and I follow, closing it behind us. There's no coat on the hook by the door. "Kjell?" I call, but the word falls flat. Liv doesn't say anything. I don't know what to do, but she seems to. She walks into the room, approaches the coffee table. With one finger she spreads the magazines out to see what they are. *Sports Illustrated, The Economist*. I follow her to the kitchen area where, with the same probing finger, she pulls open the cabinets and looks silently inside. Is she nodding? She opens the fridge. She bends over and lets her eyes roam over everything there. In the bedroom we have to turn on the light. The bed is precisely made, the bedspread navy blue and white stripes. There are no photos on the bedside table, only a lamp and a book in Norwegian. Liv flips through it and puts it down again. On the bureau there is half a roll of mints and a pair of cufflinks.

When Liv opens the closet I smell his cologne. I wait for Liv to react. She doesn't. She leads on in silence to the bathroom, turning on the light outside the door. He's making do with an old shower curtain, cracked at the top and mildewed along the bottom. The towels look new, though. Liv doesn't take the whole bathroom in, but investigates the medicine cabinet, just as Morten did when I showed him our own bathroom. There's not much in his: cologne, extra soap, eye drops, shaving cream and razor, toothpaste and toothbrush. With the one finger she has been using throughout the house, she touches the toothpaste tube. It's not a brand I recognize. In the first words she has spoken since the shouting in the car, she says, "He refuses to use anything else."

We stand in the bathroom for a while longer and I start focusing more determinedly on the details. The bathmat is crooked; he closes the toilet cover. Looking at the mirror, I focus away from our reflection – two such needy people – and look at the mirror's surface instead. There are a few white splotches, probably from vigorous tooth-brushing. There are a few fingerprints. Right next to these are something I don't recognize. I lean over the sink to look more closely. A dozen or so tiny, stiff black hairs are stuck to the mirror, spread out over a few square inches.

"What are you looking at?"

"I don't know. What do you think these are?"

I move over so Liv can look. "Eyebrow hairs," she says.

"Really?"

"Really."

"What are they doing there?"

"Waiting to be cleaned off."

"Yeah, but how did they get there?"

"Like this," says Liv, pulling her right eyebrow up with her left hand, and making pincers of her right thumb and forefinger. She pretends to pull a hair with the imaginary tweezers, and then blows the hair off them. Straight at the mirror.

"That doesn't make any sense."

"Yes it does. The base of the hair is very sticky. It sticks to the tweezers, that's why you have to blow it off. Then it sticks to the mirror."

"I understand. But Morten . . . Kjell is blond. Whose eyebrow hairs are these?" The answer comes to me as I'm asking the question. But I say nothing. The sound of a car door brings us back out of the bathroom to the living room. I look outside with my heart pounding in my throat, but it's just a neighbor. I return to the bathroom and the bedroom to turn off the lights. Back in the kitchen, Liv is looking in the fridge again. "He doesn't like skim milk," she says.

I know who does, though.

At home, Liv sits in the bedroom chair, chewing on a thumbnail. She looks intense, and highly motivated. To do what? "Do you want to talk?" I ask her, but she doesn't hear me.

In the study, I call Noriko. She's not home. I call the hospital and leave a message, and stare at the books on the shelves without moving until she calls me back.

Without preamble, I say, "I didn't realize how far things had gone with Morten. Kjell."

"He told you?" she says.

"I saw your skim milk in his fridge."

Another person might start dissembling here, saying that was nothing to base assumptions on. But Noriko says, sadly, "The best nights of my life."

"But you haven't been over there since Liv remembered who he is, right?"

Silence.

"You have?"

She exhales loudly, then says quietly, "Every single spare minute I can find, I spend with him."

"Why?"

"I can't help it."

"Noriko, I need you to stay away from him right now."

"Are you sure?"

"I can't believe this. Liv's amnesia was something to do with him. She's *traumatized*, Nori."

"I know. I know. But, maybe I can help find stuff out."

"Don't do it, please. Tell him . . . tell him you'd like to take a break until Liv has stabilized and things are clearer. It's a reasonable request."

"He'll tell me I don't trust him."

"Wow, Noriko. He's really got you where he wants you."

"That's not fair, Leo. What if he's got me where *I* want me?"

"Why isn't he creeping you out at all?"

"I don't know. He isn't, okay? He just isn't."

I breathe. "Up to you, then. Be our friend, or be Kjell's lover. *Kjell's* lover. Not Morten's. Morten is gone. We don't know Kjell. I leave it up to you."

"*Leo*," she whines, and I hang up.

. . .

I switch on the red light in my darkroom and pop my film out of its cartridges. Unrolling the first roll onto a spiral, I wonder what it would have meant for Liv and me if Morten had never arrived, or if I hadn't taken her to my photography class. I let my mind wander along these paths until I've developed a contact sheet of all the shots on the first roll. I hang it to dry and turn on the brighter light to consider which ones to blow up. Four look interesting, and I get them ready for the enlarger. I turn on the red light again. There's a lot of waiting involved, a lot of wondering, a lot of feeling alone and strangely lit. My hands never look like my own down here. I'm the ghoul in the basement. Images begin to emerge from the paper in the developing tray. Dark gray patterns, words, twists and flaps delineate patches of white. As the first photo clarifies itself I realize it is the reverse of what I imagined it would be. Instead of showing the slow covering up of discarded objects by the snow, the trash appears to be emerging from it.

When I get upstairs, Liv is in the kitchen. She tells me Karin is home, upstairs changing. Liv looks tired. "How are you feeling?" I ask her.

"I'm glad you came up. I couldn't imagine where you were, and I didn't know what to do about dinner."

"Anything is fine."

"Anything is too difficult."

"Soup from a can, then. I'll take care of it."

The silence is almost comfortable. I wonder if I can feel optimistic, standing close to Liv, opening the cans and stirring the soup. We both tense up when Karin enters. She's followed by a wave of fragrance.

"You smell lovely," I tell her.

"I thought a little scent might brighten up the evening."

She's looking at Liv. "Do you remember this one, Livvie? You used to borrow it all the time. So sweet, little girls in perfume."

"I remember," says Liv, but she's not smiling, and she's not looking at her mother.

"Is it a nice memory, Liv?" Karin asks.

Liv's eyes fill with tears. "It is," she says simply. It seems like the perfect moment for the two women to approach each other, but neither moves. Even when Liv looks across at her mother's face, Karin doesn't take it as an invitation. She just nods. Conveniently the soup threatens to boil over.

After the meal I tell them I'd like to show them my new photos, and bring up the four I've blown up to eight by twelve. I lay them on the kitchen counter because they're still a bit tacky. Karin studies them carefully and declares them poignant. Liv says, "Very nice, Leo," and squeezes my arm. She leaves the room, no doubt to go to bed.

When she's gone, Karin asks, "Doesn't anyone in this house care how things are in the pewter business these days?"

"Doesn't seem like it, does it?"

"Not even you?"

"Yeah. I suppose you should get me up to date, especially if you're having any problems. But I trust you."

"Good. There's a fax I don't understand. I'll get it."

She turns to leave the room and I say, "I mean, basically I trust you."

Karin turns back. "But what?" she asks flatly.

"Well." I clear my throat. "When Morten, Kjell, arrived, he told me he had learned our address from you."

"But he didn't. I told you on the phone."

"How did he find out where Liv lived, then?"

Karin doesn't move.

I pursue the subject. "I wonder why he said that."

"He seems to lie a lot."

"Do you think he does it for fun?"

Karin looks around the room. "I don't know. Why do any of us lie?" She shakes her head and turns again toward the living room, looking exhausted. "I wish I had my guitar here," she mumbles as she goes.

I stare at my photos on the table. "Poignant." "Nice." I want to show them to Morten. Morten would have had lots to say.

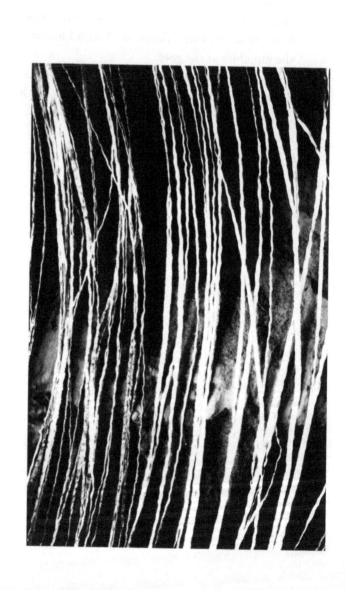

SIXTEEN

Very early on Thursday morning, before getting into my boots, I sit at the kitchen table and watch the second hand go around the face of my watch. Its movement means nothing to me. The house is quiet, and time seems to be standing still. I guess I zone out for a bit. Maybe I'm gathering myself together. I don't know why I think I'll be any more successful than usual at dealing with Kjell this time. I can't be sure. The thing I do know is that if I am unsuccessful today, I will stop trying.

There's an inch of snow on the ground. I take note of the shiny new snow shovel propped by the side of Kjell's front step. It looks very optimistic. I open the storm door as Kjell opens the inside door. The confrontation could begin here. I get the feeling that he would like to exchange a meaningful look over the threshold, but I avoid locking eyes with him by stepping inside and taking off my boots.

"It's like Norway out there," he says as I drape my coat over the back of a chair.

"Let's sit down," I respond.

He spreads his arms. "As you wish."

I sit in the one armchair and watch him choose a position, remembering how comfortable he was in my house on that first day, lounging on my furniture, telling his lies. He sits on the couch, leaning forward with his elbows on his knees, seeking my eyes with his, trying to look helpful. I sit back, as far as possible from his sphere of influence. I keep my voice level: "What are you doing here?"

He looks around the room, all wide-eyed and innocent.

"Cut it out," I say.

His eyes snap back to me. "Okay," he says. "Okay. I'm going to be honest with you, Leo."

I cross my arms.

"I wanted to see Liv," he says. "I wanted to be sure she was okay."

"Why didn't you think she was okay?"

He examines his fingernails. I know I'm going to wonder if he's lying, no matter what comes out of his mouth. Finally he puts his hand back on his thigh and looks at me decisively. "I saw her in Oslo."

This news makes me squint. It's like he's yanked a nose hair. "You mean, when she was just there?"

"Yes."

"What do you mean you saw her?"

"I saw her. I was sitting at a café and I saw her walking across the square."

"And?"

"I went over to her."

I couldn't have imagined this. I'm hardly breathing. "And?"

"It was strange. She had trouble talking to me."

"You're surprised?"

"A little, but I agree that was amazing, both of us being in that square in Oslo at the same time." His eyes soften as he remembers this, and he's wearing the stubbornly astonished expression of people who talk about Fate. "But she just seemed shocked rather than amazed. Nothing I was saying was reaching her. So I stopped asking her questions and started telling her about me, and how I'd moved to the States."

"Did she respond to that?"

Kjell slows down. "She didn't say anything, Leo. She fainted."

There's a tingling in my face. "She fell?"

"I couldn't catch her. One second she was standing, the next she was on the ground."

"What did you do?"

"I started calling out, asking if there was a nurse or a doctor around, and a couple of people came over. There was a woman, a doctor, she turned Liv on her side and Liv woke up. She was pale and sweaty, but she said she was fine. The doctor gave me her number, told me maybe Liv should have a brain scan, which seemed silly, so I took Liv to her hotel. I made her some tea."

"What was the conversation like then?"

"Really weird, but, I guess you'd say was friendly. She looked out the window, mostly. We talked about the weather. She was so sweet, so grateful. She hugged me. I made sure she was lying down when I left."

"Did you see her again after that?"

He shakes his head. "I went to her hotel in the morning, but she wasn't there. They told me she was checking out the next day. I didn't realize she was leaving so soon."

"So you followed."

"I got on the first plane I could."

"So you should have been here after her, but you arrived before her."

He shrugs. "I don't know what happened. It was very confusing."

My muscles are in knots. I have to get up. I walk to the opposite wall and turn. "You said it was Karin who told you where we lived, but it was Liv?"

He shakes his head. "I read the address on her luggage tag, when I was in her hotel room." I wonder if this admission of sneakiness is designed to throw me off the scent of a bigger one. He looks chastened, but I don't know. He could be laughing at me inside.

"I don't believe you came here to see if she was okay," I tell him.

"I did," he replies, but I stare at him until he adds, "Sort of."

"You wanted Liv to go away with you."

He looks away.

"Right?"

"Guilty," he says quietly.

"Weren't you worried that when you came and introduced yourself as her half-brother named Morten, Liv would deny what you were saying?"

He shrugs. "I took a chance."

"Why?"

"I felt pretty sure that Liv would go along with it."

"*Why?*"

He shrugs again.

"It's not going to happen, Kjell."

"I know," he says.

"So you can go now. Go away."

"But I can still help."

"Help Liv? Or help you?"

"Help . . . the situation."

"Liv's? That's a laugh. Karin's? You should see her. She's a wreck. And did you think for a second about *my* situation? Christ, man, you go around like some puppeteer, pulling strings. Or, no, like some film editor, hacking at the reel until it's in shreds. Now what are you going to do, try and splice it back together the way that suits you?"

He sits back. I can't believe he's beginning to look amused. He raises his eyebrows as if to say, *Very impressive. I didn't know you had it in you.* The diabolical thing is that I didn't know I had it in me either, and a part of me appreciates his reaction. For fuck's sake. I take a deep breath and let it out through my nose, pick up my coat and put it on. He gets up. I put my hand on the doorknob. I feel frustrated and angry. I'm going away with some of what I need but there's a lot I feel I'm leaving behind.

"I liked Morten so much," I tell him.

He smiles sadly. "So did I."

"Stay away from Liv. Stay away from all of us."

"I won't promise, Leo. I know I can help."

"Go away," I say again, and leave the house.

I have a class to teach. Maybe I can manage teaching today since there's no content to prepare; we'll just be critiquing the students' night shots. They'll ask me how the woman who threw up at the back of the class is. I'll tell them she's fine. I'll tell them to watch out for the cafeteria clam chowder or something.

Liv comes into the kitchen in her pajamas and slippers as I'm putting some fruit in my backpack.

"Where are you going?" she asks.

"To the college."

"Have you had breakfast?" She looks like she hopes I haven't.

"Yes," I say.

"Oh," she says. Tiny voice.

"Your mom should be up soon."

"I want *you*," she says, and I go to her and take her in my arms. "I have to tell you some things," she says.

"It's okay," I tell her. "I know you saw Kjell in Oslo."

She pushes me away, hard, and her hands fly to her gaunt cheeks.

"It's *okay*," I say again.

"It's very not okay," she says.

"You fainted, right?"

She drops her hands. "Fainted?"

"Kjell says you fainted in the square."

"No, Leo, no. I did not faint."

"When he told you he had moved to the States?"

"What? No. That's not what he told me."

"In the square? Did you meet by chance in a square?"

"Yes. A square."

"And he was in a café, and saw you walking—"

"No! He told you this?"

I am such a chump. "Yes."

"No, Leo. God. I wanted to do this, I don't know, calmly. Sitting down." She comes back to me and takes my hands in her icy ones. "Can we sit down?" She takes a step backward, pulling me with her. "Can we sit on the couch?"

I have to go but I nod.

When we're on the couch Liv starts to cry. She lets go of my hands to put them on her face, and doubles over. I rub her back. Her emotional pain is physical; it's the severest physical pain I've ever seen.

"Oh," Karin says from the doorway, and Liv suddenly sits up, face blotchy, and looks from Karin to me.

"Liv wants to tell me something," I explain to Karin, hoping she'll go away again.

"Not like this," Liv says. She submits to a sob, then gets up. She whispers, "I will try again later," and jogs across the room, brushing past her mother to get to the stairs.

Karin and I look at each other, both obviously waiting for the other to speak. I go ahead. "Something's coming."

Karin folds her arms, nods, but doesn't reply. I get up.

"I'm going to class," I tell her. "Home as soon as I can." She follows me to the kitchen.

Before I go out the door I say, "Try to get her to eat something. She needs strength." Again she nods. I wonder when she'll unfold her arms.

No one is downstairs when I get home. I experience a jolt of fear that I've been abandoned, and once I'm out of my coat I hurry to the stairs. From halfway up I can see that the guest room door is open. From the top I can see that ours is still closed. Karin sits on a chair in the corner of the guest room. She has found the knitting supplies Liv keeps in the deep bottom drawer of the chest and is clicking away at something the color of oatmeal. She looks up and gives me a tense smile.

"Has she come out?" I ask.

"No."

"Did she eat, though?"

"Yes. Cheese on toast, and a banana."

I nod. "Okay. How about you?"

"A banana. My stomach is too tight for eating."

"Well, I need some lunch." I go to our bedroom door and tap gently.

"Who is it?" Liv calls out.

"It's Leo. May I come in?"

"Yes."

For once the TV isn't on. I had expected her to be under the covers, but she's sitting, dressed, on the edge of the made bed. I smell shampoo, and her hair is fluffy, so it seems she has pulled herself together, had a shower and dried her hair.

"Want to come downstairs?" I ask her.

She nods and gets up. I let her leave the bedroom before me, and she goes straight down the stairs without stopping to glance in the guest room. She stops in the middle of the living room.

"Maybe sit down?" Liv says, so I go to the couch and sit. Liv remains standing, trying to decide where to put her hands. They go into her jeans pockets and come back out, hide behind her back and then slide into her pockets again.

"I saw Kjell in Oslo," she says.

"Yes," I say. "He told me."

Liv says, "We met by chance."

"Are you sure it was chance?"

"Oh," she says quietly, disturbed, and looks at the carpet. "I don't know." After a moment she looks up and says, "I can't think about that. That's too many things to think about. Okay? We met in Oslo. Somehow. I don't know how. Okay?"

"Of course. Sorry."

"And then . . . Leo . . . Leo . . ." Some awful feeling is squeezing her face. She comes and kneels in front of me. "It was such a shock, Leo. It was . . . crazy. It wasn't real. He looked different, but he felt the same."

"Felt?"

"I mean, I remembered him. His whole . . . atmosphere." Her face has cleared a little. It is pale, overall, but there's a pink bloom on her cheeks as she describes the reunion. "It was incredible. I didn't believe it, but I had to believe it also, and I finally had the chance to ask him why he had disappeared." She looks as if she's waiting for me to say that I'm happy for her. I'm about to go ahead and say it, even though I don't know how I feel, but then Karin appears in the doorway. "What did he tell you?" she demands.

Liv looks behind her at her mother and tells her to go away.

"No."

Liv turns back to me, looks at my knees, thinks. "Okay," she says, sounding resigned. "Sit and listen if you have to. It's okay. I won't have to do this twice. But I have to say it like it happened."

"Why?" asks Karin sharply.

"Can we let Liv do this her way?" I ask her. "Come and sit down." I recognize she's in pain too. We're all in pain. It might be one of the worst days of all our lives. I'm reasonably sure Liv's pain wins, though.

Karin sits.

Liv looks at me again. She puts her hands on my knees as if she isn't sure she's allowed to.

"I slept with him, Leo," Liv whispers.

"Yes, I know," I tell her, gently, as if gentleness could stop what she is about to clarify.

"In *Oslo*, Leo."

Karin bellows. No words come out of her mouth, only

sound, the kind of sound I imagine a mother would make if she had just learned her child was dead. I look from her to Liv to see if Liv understands why Karin feels so wounded, when I'm the one who has been betrayed. She does. "Leo," she says, but Karin jumps to her feet shouting, "No! Don't!"

I want to shut Karin out. She is a raging storm. I want to look at Liv and know exactly what I'm seeing, but I can't. When she takes my hands I let her. My hands stay slack as Liv tightens her grip on them and pulls me forward to speak into my ear while Karin continues to shout, now in Norwegian. I'm afraid Karin's going to lunge, to try to pull us apart. Liv presses her cheek to mine and tells me Kjell is her half-brother.

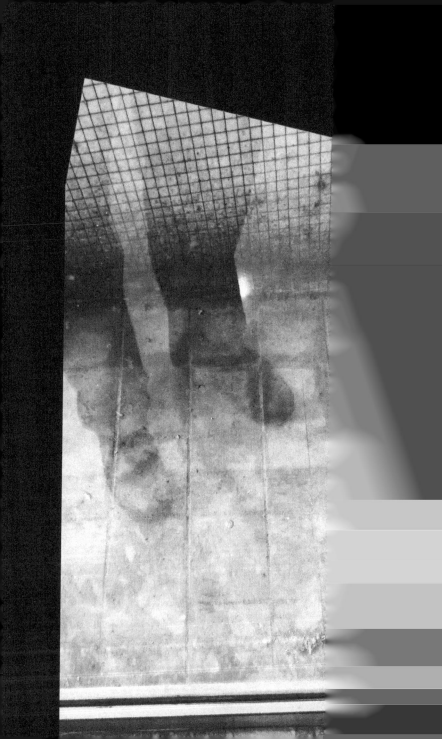

SEVENTEEN

I can't move. Liv is squeezing my hands rhythmically like she's hoping it will keep my heart beating. Her face is desperate. Karin continues her anguished shouting until she sees Liv has said what she intended to say, and then we're all quiet. Liv's hands keep squeezing mine, sporadically now, like a dog scratching at a door, listening for signs of life, scratching again. My brain struggles from "I slept with him, Leo" to "Kjell *is* my half-brother." I part my lips and Liv's hands go still.

I whisper, "He wasn't lying."

Liv nods, and her lip trembles.

"All lies, except that one?"

"Yes."

"When did you learn this?"

"He told me after we slept together."

I'm listening to us whisper to each other. I'm seeing us in profile as if from the end of the couch: me sitting, slumped; Liv crouching, alert, terrified; Karin standing, feet planted wide apart, trying to stabilize herself, or make herself feel bigger, to have more influence.

"Why did he do that to you?" I whisper, and Liv's eyes lose the shape of terror, recognizing that what I have just said sounds like solidarity. Maybe it is. I'm too wound up in trying to understand Kjell's motivation right now to open my mind fully to the fact that at some time in the last two weeks my wife wasn't able to resist him. Did telling her they were actually siblings occur to him in the post-coital glow, or did he plan it beforehand? Did he really run into her by chance? How long has he really known he and Liv are siblings?

I feel my brain click back on. I look at Karin. She tips her chin up, expecting an attack.

"Morten said," I start. "*Kjell* said that he had learned about Liv from their father."

Karin just stares at me, waiting for the question.

"He didn't, did he?"

Now Liv is looking at Karin too. Karin eventually shakes her head.

I move my hands to cover Liv's and she and I look in each other's eyes. I wait to see if she'll draw the conclusion I have. Her forehead descends, then rises above her shocked eyes. She turns back to Karin. "*You* told him?"

Karin's fingers are tearing at each other. I'm sure she's not the enemy. I know she loves her daughter, and that her love isn't the wretched, twisted thing that Kjell has abused Liv with. "Come and sit, Karin," I say, and she steps to the couch. As she sits down on my left she emits a sob, just the one, before breathing deeply to steady herself. I pull Liv up to sit next to me on the other side, and we wait.

"I told him," Karin eventually says, to her thighs.

"When?" Liv demands.

"When you got pregnant."

Liv thinks for a long moment, then asks, "But how did *you* know?"

"Your father. Tor told me. He called me. You remember you met him? When you announced you were pregnant and he came to Bergen?"

"Of course. Yes. Lunch."

"Yes."

"He left early."

"Yes, when he realized who the father was, and he called me."

Liv thinks. Shakes her head. "Why didn't you tell *me*?"

"Perhaps the same reason Tor didn't tell Kjell. We were cowards. We wanted it all just to go away. We wanted never to have to tell our children what they were doing. And when you were so sure you wanted a baby at seventeen, and I couldn't change your mind at all, I told Kjell. Just in case *he* would do the right thing. I had hoped he would tell you, and you would come to the decision together."

"But he didn't."

"No, he didn't."

"He disappeared instead."

Karin nods. "We didn't know him."

We sit in silence.

We aren't hungry, but Karin reasserts her role as mother by going to the kitchen and clinking around. She comes back with a bowl of nuts and three glasses in her long hands, a bottle of ginger ale under her arm. We aren't hungry, but we reach for the nuts, and we drink. The ginger ale tastes fantastic on my dry tongue. Liv is staring at her mother with the same intensity she had when we brought Karin home from the airport. This time I can see her brain is putting the pieces together rather than searching for the pieces. It seems to make Karin feel shy. "What shall we do?" she asks, but as she does, Liv gets up and crosses in front of me to climb on her mother's lap. She doesn't just sit on Karin's thighs, she pulls her feet up onto the couch and turns her body to bury her face in her mother's neck. They put their arms around each other, and no one answers Karin's question yet. Liv's gesture feels like an apology, or maybe a thank you. It feels like a re-set. So much has gone unsaid in this family, but in this moment words are unnecessary. I wonder if Liv will make a similar gesture toward me. I'll need one. I'll need words, too.

When Karin and Liv have had their fill, Liv gets up off her mother's lap. There's a knock on the door. Liv freezes and we all look at each other. "Oh, no," Liv says. "We're not ready."

"Might not be him," I say, although I realize I've grabbed the edge of the couch.

"What if it is?" Karin asks.

"We can play it by ear," I say.

The knock comes again.

"Stay here," I tell them. "I'll go."

Walking through to the kitchen I'm sure it will be Kjell, but it's Alice Fulsom's face behind the glass of the storm door. I've never been this close to her.

"Oh!" I say, pushing the door open. Under other circumstances I'd be confused by the arrival of Alice, but today I'm so relieved she's not Kjell that my welcome probably sounds out of sync. "Come in!"

"Are you sure?" she asks, her Massachusetts accent heavy, rasped by cigarettes.

"Of course, of course. Come in."

She places her huge hands on the doorframe and heaves her bulk into the house. Her profile, as it passes me, is liver-splotched and dotted with hanging moles. She smells of smoke and wool. Her open tent of a parka looks like a hand-me-down from a man.

"I just wanted to thank you, really," she says. "For raking."

"Sure," I say. "Come on through."

"Well, okay," she says, and follows me. "I know you've done it twice," she says to my back.

"It's Alice," I tell Karin and Liv as the old woman lumbers into the living room. No doubt they're also relieved it wasn't Kjell at the door, but Liv gives me a look of surprise — not so much at Alice's arrival as at the fact that I'm guiding her to an armchair when we have so much to discuss. What am I doing? I'm not sure what I'm doing; I'm only sure I want to do it. Maybe I want someone else to talk with for a little while – a human barrier between the three of us and whatever is going to happen next.

"Oh, that's nice," Alice says as she settles into the chair. "I'd forgotten chairs could be other shapes than my old chairs."

We laugh at this honest reference to her solitary life — Alice's laugh sounds like the growl of a guard dog — and Liv says, "Glass of ginger ale, Alice?"

"Sure," Alice says. "Thank you kindly."

Liv jumps up to get a glass.

"I like the ceiling light," Alice says, having looked around the room. "Got it from a castle or something?"

"Nothing so fancy," I say, "but we paid a king's ransom to ship it from Norway."

"Christ," she says, and then Liv is back and pouring for her. She accepts the glass with thanks, and drinks, and smacks her lips. "Norway, huh? That where you're from?" She's looking at Liv.

"Yes," Liv says. "And this is my mother."

"Thought so," says Alice. "Visiting?"

"Yes," Karin says.

"What about the guy with the food?"

We're not sure who's going to answer this, or how. I say, "Oh, you noticed him?"

Alice smiles. "Of course. What do you think I do all day? Cavort?"

We laugh harder this time, and Alice drinks again, stopping to growl a little, her big belly jumping, clearly enjoying herself.

"Anyway," she says. "Who is he?"

"My half-brother," Liv answers bravely.

Alice rests her eyes on Liv. After a while she says, "Doesn't look like you."

Liv is uncomfortable. It flashes through my mind that if Kjell and Liv resembled each other more we might not be in this situation. Someone might have suspected right away. But maybe not. Lots of people choose partners who look like themselves.

Alice adds, "Looks like an asshole, pardon my French."

Again we're laughing, and it's like Alice has taken the lid off the pressure cooker we're in and we can feel a little fresh air and light. The situation is simple: Kjell's an asshole.

"Yeah," I say. "He is."

. . .

Waving goodbye to Alice once I've seen her to her door, I imagine inviting her to ours for Christmas. That could be fun. When I turn around and start walking home, I keep smiling because Liv is waiting for me behind the storm door, arms crossed to keep warm, but I feel the darkness descend again. I have to keep smiling. My wife is waiting for me. Will she be with me at Christmas, though? What does she hope for now? What do I want?

Back in the kitchen we stand facing each other. When she doesn't say anything right away I hang up my coat, then resume my position three feet from her.

"Where's Karin?" I ask.

"I asked her to go upstairs."

I nod.

"I think," Liv says, "I think that you should ask me all your questions."

"Oh. Are you sure?"

"Yes. I want to get everything out today."

"I doubt that's possible."

"Leo, stop it. Don't doubt. Let's do this."

"Here?"

"Yes. Right here. She'll hear us if we go to the living room."

"We could go out."

"*Ask*, Leo. *Please*."

"Okay." I take a deep breath. "Did you *try* to resist him?"

"This is a good question. I don't think there was time to try."

"No time to try? No *time*? What, you bump into him and drop to the ground and have sex right there on the sidewalk? What do you *mean* no time?"

She drops her head.

"There was time to consider," I insist. "I'm sure there was."

Head still low, she nods.

"Just no desire to."

"I'm so sorry," she whispers.

"He's. . . Look . . . It's *not* okay. But he's a tidal wave. I get that."

She looks up again. "I feel I am punching you," she says.

"You are."

She starts to unfold her arms, maybe to extend her hands to me, but thinks better of it and keeps holding on to herself. She says, "Next question?"

I can't speak.

"The questions will poison you if you don't ask. I know this," she says.

I also know this.

"So," I say, looking briefly in her eyes, looking away again, "if he hadn't told you that you were related, would you have left me?"

"I don't know."

"So, he could have had you?"

"Maybe."

"Then why did he tell you? Did he want to hurt you?"

"No."

"He must have," I insist. "There's no other — "

"He thought I knew."

I don't breathe for a second, then inhale. "He thought you knew, and that you were fine with it?"

"Yes."

"So fine with it that he thought he could come here and get you?"

"Yes, I guess that's right."

"Wait, couldn't he tell you weren't fine with it after he told you?"

"I guess not."

"Why not?" I bring my voice back down. "How did you react?"

Her shoulders go up. "I'm having some trouble remembering that part."

"Please don't lie to me, Liv."

"I'm not." Her eyes well up. "I can't . . ." She has to take a few breaths. "I can't remember that part. I was with him. Then I was somewhere in Grünerløkka."

"Where is that?"

"Closer to the river."

"Still in Oslo."

"Yes. It was very dark, and quiet."

"Some time had passed, you mean?"

"Lots of time. But I only know that now. Right then, I was just lost."

"You remembered that you were staying at the hotel, though?"

"That's where my feet took me."

"That's weird."

"Like a dream."

"And you changed your ticket."

"I had to think."

"And then I called and left a message."

She nods. "Thank God. Then I knew what to do."

"But you left the Bondeheimen."

"Yes."

"The day *before* you flew home."

"I did?"

"Where did you go that night?"

She blinks.

"You called me from a payphone."

She still doesn't speak.

"Do you not remember that?"

"I don't." Saying this seems to hurt her. Her wan face is tense, her eyes frightened. She looks around the kitchen and then she clears her throat.

"Can we go back to the part where I knew I had a husband so I knew what to do?"

"Okay."

"Can we stay at that part? I don't remember the rest."

The look on her face makes me want to pull her to me, but I have to ask, "Is there any part of you that is okay with the fact that he is your brother?"

"No," she replies, very firmly.

Tears come to my eyes. "Are you completely sure, Liv? Do you not love him at all?"

She takes a long time to respond. I usually like it when people take time to think, but not this time. While I wait the tears spill over and my nose starts to run.

"What is love?" she says.

At first I think this is the first line of some kind of speech, but she's really asking me. I wipe my nose on my wrist. "Seriously?"

"Yes. Very seriously."

"Um, okay. Is it attachment? Extreme attachment?"

Liv thinks again. "No. That could be like an addiction, right?"

"I guess."

"It's more fondness, maybe," she says. "Extreme fondness?"

"That doesn't sound very sexy."

"It is, though."

I don't know what to say.

Liv speaks again. "I'm not fond of Kjell. I *was* attached. Attached like addicted. Seeing him again made me crazy, and then it made me sick. It still makes me sick."

"Do you want to see him anymore?"

"No."

"You wanted to go to his house."

"I wanted to kill him."

"And now?"

"Now I am tired. It's enough, now. We need to rest."

"He's still here, though."

She nods. "This is where we need a plan."

I nod.

"Do you have more questions, Leo?"

I do. I have a question I don't want to have to ask. I start to cry again, damn it, and Liv understands me. She uncrosses her arms and takes my hands. "I love you, Leo," she says. "I love you. I love you. I love you. I love you. I love — "

I stop her with a hug.

I think she's telling the truth.

I hope.

EIGHTEEN

Karin starts a stew, sweating onions and searing beef in an obvious effort to give us our appetites back. She has poured us each a small glass of red wine, but is guarding the rest of the bottle to pour in the pot. Noriko arrives. I left a message for her at the hospital, and she has hurried over after her shift. We need a hearty meal, and clearly Noriko does too. I've never seen her face so pale. She's never presented anything but a smile upon arriving in our kitchen. She and Liv go to the living room together while Karin and I keep working on dinner. I want to hear their conversation, but they need to reconnect and I should let them. I measure out some rice and suddenly I wonder when I will ever find the right moment to talk to Liv about the boys. It's days since I've thought about them, and doing so is a welcome reunion. It was what I was doing before all this shit hit the fan. Given what I've learned about Svendsen family secrets, I may have grounds to hope that Liv will be forgiving. We'll be even. If that's how it works with secrets.

By the time we sit down to eat, Noriko knows what Liv

has revealed. The stew is fantastic, but it's a subdued scene. We talk briefly about beef versus reindeer meat. Reindeer is much leaner. "Just like Norwegians," Noriko says, and then the conversation dies again. It's uncomfortable not to be talking, but it's comfortable that we're together. There's safety in the numbers of our tiny army.

I clear my throat, gathering six beautiful eyes my way. "I know you don't want to see him again, Liv," I say, "and you don't have to, but I feel like we need to get him out of town."

Liv stops chewing, starts again.

"I don't want him coming here," I continue, "and I can absolutely see him doing that. He'll get frustrated, our silence will make him crazy, and he'll come. So I think we should go and tell him to leave. I've already told him once, and I'll go alone again if I have to, but a united front might be better."

Karin puts down her fork. "He has tried to divide us, so if we're together, he will know he can't do that."

Liv puts her fork down too. "I don't want to," she says.

"Okay," I say, although I'm disappointed. "Noriko?"

"I'm in," Noriko says.

Karin picks up her fork again. "Eat up," she says. "Eat it all up."

"So basically," I say across the open dishwasher to Karin and Noriko, "the message is a unified 'Get out of here.' Whatever he says, we return to that?"

"Worth a try," Noriko says.

"Until we have a reason to call the police," Karin says.

"Hoping to avoid that," I say.

Liv, still at the table, doesn't speak.

Kitchen tidied, three of us put on our coats.

Then four.

"Oh," I say, as Liv zips herself in.

"This won't work if I don't come too. He won't believe you."

The thought had crossed my mind. I don't want her to suffer, though. "I don't want you to suffer," I tell her.

She shrugs. "You are trying to help me. So I will try to help you."

Unlocking the car I look at the women standing on either side of it, and the vapor coming from their mouths gives me an image of a cartoon bull pawing the ground, nostrils steaming. We're tense during the drive.

"I don't think we should go inside," I say.

"Agreed," Liv says immediately.

"What if he's not there?" Noriko asks.

"Where else would he be?" Karin asks back. "Does he know anyone else?"

We crunch to a stop in front of the house. There is no car on the driveway, no light over the door or shining between the parted curtains. When I came here alone this morning I didn't notice the Christmas decorations on the house next door, but all the colorful fairy lights are on now, and a three-foot plastic snowman glows at the corner of the house, looking pleased with himself. By contrast, Kjell's house looks more than dark. It looks dead.

"No Kjell," says Liv.

"We better be sure," Noriko replies.

We all get out and troop up the path and onto the empty flowerbed in front of the living-room window, then take turns cupping our hands around our faces to look in. The Christmas tree is gone. Everything is gone.

We huddle on the small snow-covered lawn. Someone passing might take us for carolers deciding where to go next.

"I didn't see that coming," says Noriko. "I thought he'd fight."

"Where has he gone?" asks Karin.

"We don't even know where he came from," I say.

Then Liv says, "Thank you, Leo," and steps over to embrace me. I wrap my arms around her and lean my cheek on her head. I can feel this sight warming Noriko and Karin's hearts, and for their benefit and Liv's I breathe a deep sigh. Silently, though, I don't think I've done anything to be thanked for. Morten is gone for good, but Kjell is only gone from this house. He's still hiding behind something, somewhere on the planet, maybe even in Bridgewater. He's not just an asshole. He's insane.

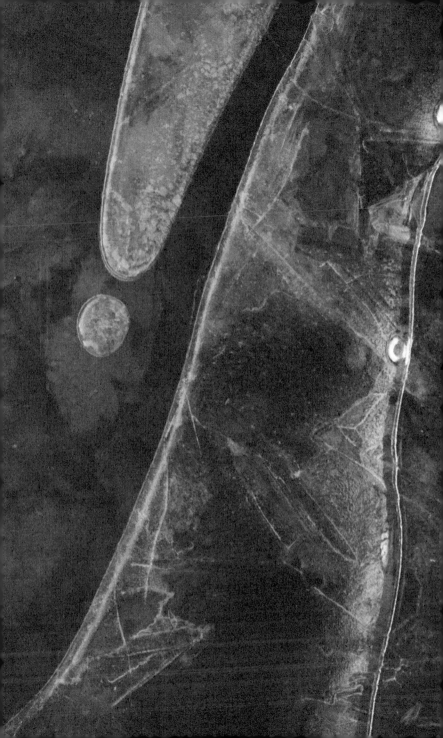

NINETEEN

I make myself drive by Kjell's house at least once a day for the next few days. The curtains never change position. There's never a light on. Even so, my heart pounds as I pass by. One day I drive by three times, just in case I surprise him returning to the scene of the crime. Finally it occurs to me to call his number, and it has been disconnected. I tell Liv he's really gone, and I think she looks reassured.

Karin goes too. She didn't want to leave before Kjell had cleared out, but she needs to get back to gigging. She has no income otherwise, and her agent has been calling.

The hug Liv gives her mother at the airport is different from any hug I've seen her give her in the past. It's not the perfunctory hug I was used to before the amnesia, and it's not the excited, childish hug Karin received upon arrival. It's long. They drop their heads against each other. They soak each other up.

Once we've waved Karin off, Liv turns to me and puts her forehead against my sweater, holding on to my open coat for support, pulling down on it as her shoulders shake with emotion. I want to soothe her but I don't know if soothing is what is called for. Eventually her shoulders settle. She opens her fists and lays her hands flat on my chest, and then looks up at me. Blotchy. Snotty. Beautiful. Mine?

"We can go visit her soon," I say, in case that's anywhere near what she needs me to say.

She shakes her head. "No. No, no. I won't be going to Norway for a while. No, it's just . . . I think it's just . . . Well . . . I feel . . . Maybe I'm allowed to love her again." Then she slides her hands down into my coat pockets, hunting for tissues. She remembers I always keep some there. This simple intimacy hurts my chest.

"Oh God, Liv, I love you so much I could crack."

She pulls her hands out, tissue in one, and smiles sadly at me. She blows her nose.

"Are we going to be okay?" I ask when she's done.

"We have some work to do," she says. "I'm so sorry about that."

I shake my head, meaning she needn't apologize. We were all seduced. "We already had work to do," I tell her. "Before all this."

"We did?"

"That big fight at Christmas? Remember?"

She blinks a few times. "You want to have a baby? You want to talk about this now?"

"No, no, it's something else."

"What?" She looks on the verge of tears again.

"Okay," I say. "Not now. Come on."

I drive. Liv looks out the window.

Halfway home, she says, "What, though?"

"What?"

"What else is there you want to talk about, that we have to work on?"

"Oh."

I have to think. Do I want to tell Liv about my boys right away, after all? I promised I would say everything. I don't want to overload her and make her cry again. I want to protect her. I want to protect *us*. I know it will be a while — maybe a long time — before my love for her feels light again; it's heavy now, and painful. But in order to get there I have to know we're both being honest. I want to get everything on the table before we're in danger of returning to our previous ways. I have to teach. Liv has to get back to work and an avalanche of Christmas orders. If not now, when?

I swing off the expressway. I don't want to have this conversation at home, where it will hang in the air. I wish we could go sit by a lake, but I have to find us somewhere warm. In the end, I tell Liv about my sons in a relatively quiet corner of the food court in South Shore Plaza.

Liv has always been good at taking things in without interrupting, but I'd imagined my confession would surprise her. She's just nodding, though. Her eyes are wide, but it doesn't look like shock, or distress. Sometimes her forehead creases, but she still nods. The nods are encouraging, at least, and it's somewhat of a relief to get the story out, but it's so difficult to gauge her reaction. She doesn't seem overwhelmed at all. Maybe she's enjoying the brand-new topic of conversation, someone else's royal fuck-up. I need her to talk before I'm sure I can let go of the dread in the pit of my stomach.

Her hands have stayed on her lap. When I finish my story, she brings them up to the table and curls them around her cardboard cup of tea, and appears to study the lid. Then she says, simply and seriously, "You have to go and see them."

"Really?"

"Of course. It's terrible to think, or to *know*, that your father doesn't want you."

"Exactly. And I don't know what she tells them."

"Probably nonsense."

"I hate to think."

"But you've let her."

"Ouch."

"It's true. We have to be very real about this, Leo. You could have made an effort, but you didn't."

I look away.

"It's okay," she says. "It makes sense you did that, but they're old enough now to start imagining you. Don't let them go through that."

I let this sink in. "You'd know," I say.

"Yes."

We inhale. We exhale.

We return to our quiet house, the two of us together for the first time since she left for Norway. I call 411 and ask for the area code for Hamden, Connecticut. Once I have that, I call 555-1212 with that area code and ask for the number for Marilyn Greer at the address on the photocopy. It is given to me. Right away. My hand shakes writing it down. I don't call her. I don't want to speak to her. I don't want to alert her that I've found her. But I've found her.

Liv and I get back to work. For several days we're careful with each other. We talk about frustrating students and frustrating phone calls, and about the boys. Sometimes Liv has trouble eating. She cooks great dinners when she's the one home from work first, and cookies, too, when she needs to occupy herself. She takes only tiny servings, though, and asks me to take the cookies to work. Her face isn't filling back out after the shocks that had her lose and regain her memory. She's still seeing Ruth, and will need to keep going for a good while, I'm sure. She tells me she'll be okay, but I want to see it in her face. I want to feed her sour cream, waffles, chocolate sauce, anything to build her up. She still watches TV a lot. But she doesn't waver in her conviction that I should find the boys. We choose the Saturday on which I'll take my trip to Connecticut.

On the morning of that drive, I'm so jazzed up by the feeling that I might see them that I get up before sunrise.

"Eat," Liv says from the kitchen doorway as I'm wondering whether to wear boots or sneakers. Her face is scrunched up against the light. The rest of the house is so dark and I feel like the bright kitchen is the wheelhouse of a ship. A ship that is once again mine. I'll make this expedition and return to the ship knowing where to steer us next. I don't think it will be too difficult.

"I can't sit still long enough to eat," I tell her.

Liv smiles, sliding her hands inside the sleeves of her robe, and comes over to me. "Stop somewhere, then."

"I will. Sneakers or boots?"

"Sneakers are more comfortable to drive in."

"Yeah, and I probably won't be outside much."

I take my shoes from the back door and sit down at the table to put them on. Liv plucks affectionately at my hair. "I'm glad you're excited," she says.

"Thanks," I say, securing my laces. I go back to the door for my coat.

"When do you think you'll be back?"

"Dinnertime, latest. Very latest."

"I suddenly feel like you might not come home," she says as I start to zip up. I stop.

"Why?"

"I don't know."

She's standing right up close to me. I take her in my arms, which muffles her voice, but I hear her say, "Maybe *they're* the family you want."

"It's nothing like that," I tell her, and step back. I pull hard on the neck of my sweatshirt and the t-shirt underneath to reveal the bruised bite marks on my shoulder. "You've branded me for life."

We made love in the night, for the first time since she remembered me. I woke up to find her sliding her body onto mine. The surprise was electrifying. I don't remember our sex ever being quite that rough before. No, not rough. Strong. An effort to combine, as if crashing together would helps us understand each other. It was satisfying and unsatisfying in equal measure.

"Okay," Liv says, blushing, grinning. "Okay. You can go."

Wallet in coat pocket, keys and maps spanning from Massachusetts to New York in hand, I head out into the dark. The steps are frosty and I wheel my arms to stay upright as I clatter down them.

I hear Morten in my head. "Glide, Leo!" he shouts. "Glide!"

TWENTY

The day, when it lightens, is gray, the light weak. I listen to the radio without hearing it, frequently trapped among clusters of huge trucks, my thoughts clustering as well. I wonder if Liv has been so encouraging of my finding the boys because of what she's just been through. Would she have been so encouraging before she went to Norway? What if she had been? What if I had found them already? What if they had been at our house, baking for Liv with me, when Kjell arrived at the door as Morten? I see him at the door again, and I wonder if his shoulder had Liv's teeth marks on it then. I never saw him shirtless. I'll never know. I wish I hadn't wondered that and now I'm afraid I often will.

My thoughts eventually thin out during the second hour of trees. There's nothing to notice but where there are more trees, where fewer. Sometimes a rock formation rears up and I hear myself think *This bit is more like Norway*.

I don't stop to eat.

White picket fences begin to sprout once I've skirted New Haven. I stop once to ask directions from a man pushing a baby buggy, and then it's only a few minutes before I'm sitting in the car across the street from Marilyn's address. It's the sort of building I haven't seen much of in real life, but plenty of in TV shows, where private investigators go carefully up the long set of wooden stairs on the side that lead to a landing and a door in the wall. There's something about having to climb to the door with your shoulder to the building rather than face on that makes the approach seem less than honest. From across the street the door is flush with the cheap gray weatherboard. I get out of the car. From where I stand, the stairs go nowhere.

The street feels bare. The red tinsel on the yellow Stanley tools in the ground-floor hardware store window provide the building's only colors. It's eleven days till Christmas. I try to imagine the rooms upstairs. There must be toys, and books, and art on the walls. But maybe also curling linoleum, metal kitchen cabinets with rust around the handles.

I have the phone number, but I haven't called ahead because I didn't want Marilyn to tell me I wasn't welcome, so I don't know if anyone's home. If they're active boys, they might be out on Saturday mornings, or maybe on Saturdays they relax a little, watch cartoons, make pancakes with Marilyn.

I hesitate until I start feeling the cold of the sidewalk in the soles of my feet. I cross the street. Standing at the bottom of the stairs I feel a full-body chill. It's such a quiet street. It's such a long staircase. I have enough time on the way up to think of Kjell coming up my own stairs, and how terrible that turned out to be. But he wasn't my father. The man approaching the twins who live behind the door is their father. I'm their father. I'm their father.

A breeze rustles the remaining dry leaves on a nearby tree like nasty whispers. My legs get heavy, but then near the top I start hearing the TV. Cartoons! I was right! I arrive at the small landing. There's only the one door, no storm door. *My kids should have a storm door*, I think. It's only going to get colder. Near the top of the door are two panes of glass. A spy hole would be the better option for a woman on her own with kids. I'm embarrassed to be looking in, like a peeping Tom raised to window level on a cherry-picker. But there they are.

The shock of recognition throws off my sense of time. It's not the boys giving me the shock, though. I can't see their faces yet. It's the TV stand. It looks exactly like the wire TV stand I grew up with–rickety, on wheels, only able to support the kind of TV that gets wheeled out of the corner with reluctance and wheeled right back again. TV isn't central to my boys' upbringing, as it wasn't to mine.

One of the twins is sitting with his back to me, cross-legged in the middle of a large, braided rug, looking up at *Scooby-Doo*. His dark brown curls shine in the light from the window at the back of the building. The other boy is off to the left, at the edge of the rug, with his side to me. He's crouched over a small amount of Lego, undoing them, starting something again. His hair doesn't shine. It's like mine, a thatch. All I can hear is the TV. I listen for sounds of someone else in the rooms, but nothing comes across to me. Maybe Marilyn sleeps in on Saturdays and the boys know how to entertain themselves. They respect her wishes. Amazing. I put my left cheek against the glass to check out what room is to the right of the rug, and take in kitchen cabinets (not rusty) and a yellow, molded-plastic chair. Turning my head to look left, I see the sort of living room I expected. A two-seater sofa covered in a flag I can't identify, and a red beanbag chair. One boot on its side. Behind the TV is a doorway into a hall that ends in a bookcase. Light enters the hallway from two open doors. The bedrooms? Presumably there is a bathroom as well. I can't see a third door though. It must be closed.

I've steamed up the window. I wipe it slowly, so I don't draw attention. Both boys are transfixed, and neither moves much.

Eventually I force myself to knock. The one watching TV doesn't hear the sound, or ignores it, but the other one looks over from his Lego, curious rather than surprised. His lips are dark. Marilyn's lips. Magnets for the eye. He waits. I don't know if he can see my face so I lean right up to the glass, and smile at him. He gets up and comes to the door, opening it a little. *No!* I want to say, even as my heart lifts. *Don't open the door to a stranger!*

He opens the door only a little. I step back and down one step so that I can speak more to his level through the little gap.

"Hello. Is your mom home?"

He shakes his head.

"Where'd she go?"

"Yoga," he says.

"Do you know when she'll be back?"

"After Scooby," the boy watching TV says, loudly, to be sure I hear him without him having to turn around.

"Oh, okay. Okay then. I'll just . . .wait for her."

The boy closes the door. When I step back up to the landing and look through the window again, he's back at his Lego. I don't feel uncomfortable looking in at their life anymore. I watch the one watch TV. When Scooby and

Shaggy start running and hiding, legs going twice as fast as the mummy they're afraid of, knowing, as we all do from our dreams, that the mummy doesn't have to run to be inexorable, I watch him shift from buttock to buttock, caught up in the music. The other boy's little construction grows. He chews the inside of his cheek.

On the corner of the kitchen counter is a mug I have to stare at for a while before the pattern, which I first saw as a maple leaf, resolves into Leonardo's Vitruvian Man. I recognize that mug from Marilyn's place in Bridgewater and for a moment I feel a prickle of awkwardness again, and of misgiving, but when I look back at the boys the feeling goes away. The theme music comes on at the end of the cartoon, and I look down the stairs and out across the road to see if Marilyn is on her way. I hear the TV being turned off, and when I turn back to the door it is opening again. I step back down one step.

"Hey," I say to the shiny-haired one. "Good cartoon?"

"Yeah. Why do you want to see our mom?"

"Well," I clear my throat, "we were friends a long time ago."

"Oh," he says. His lips are paler than his brother's, his nose straight and narrow. I can't discern his eye color when he's showing me only the center third of his face in the gap. "How long?"

"Before you were born."

"What kind of friends?"

"Good friends, I guess?"

The brother with my hair pipes up. "He wants to know if you were boyfriend and girlfriend."

"Oh. Well. Yes."

The one at the door says, "Did she break your spirit?"

This makes me laugh, relieving almost all my tension.

"He means your heart," his brother corrects.

"Yes," I tell them both. "She did."

The one at the door smiles, as if he's proud of his powerful man-crushing mother.

"Does she leave you alone a lot?" I ask.

"I don't know," the boy at the door says, which doesn't make sense right away, but I then take it to mean that he doesn't know what constitutes 'a lot'.

"Okay then. Anyway. I'll just sit down here to wait. You don't have to talk to me."

I sit on the top step and look out at the road. The door closes. It's less than thirty seconds before it slowly opens again. I don't turn around. It's his turn to stare. I keep expecting Marilyn to come around the corner of the house, but I guess "after Scooby" isn't a precise time. Whichever twin is there doesn't think I'm aware of him, so he starts exaggerating his breathing to let me know. It's an invitation to look up at him, so I do. He seems happy about that, but he doesn't have anything to say.

"Don't you like Lego?" I ask the shiny-haired child.

He shakes his head, then changes his mind. "I do, but not with Leo. It's not fun."

"Leo?"

"LeoNARdo," the other boy stresses, suddenly at the door too, pushing it wider so they both can see out, and I'm looking up into both their faces. I feel giddy being looked down on by such curious little people, Leonardo and . . .

"What's *your* name then?"

"Marcus." Pronounced Markiss.

"Hey!" a woman's voice says, and I look down the stairs and stand right up because Marilyn is steaming up them in a deep-purple parka saying, "Get the hell off my stairs!" but when she's close enough to see my face she stops and puts her hands on her hips. She looks away from me to think.

I almost descend, but I stop myself. "I've met them," I say instead.

That makes her look back up. "Come down here," she says, turning around and stomping back down the stairs. She's still got the long braid. This time I obey, and follow her down to the sidewalk.

"Why now?" she asks.

"Do you mean, what took me so long?"

"Yes."

"Have you been waiting for me to come find them?"

"No. I don't know." She lifts a mittened hand to her forehead. "You could have written first. Prepared me."

"I didn't know if you'd agree."

She nods, and I relax a little. I'm about to say, "You look just the same," but suddenly she says, "I can't let you in."

"Why not?"

"I know they'll like you."

"And that's bad?"

"It might be. We don't know. I've got our little ecosystem functioning really nicely, and I don't want to disrupt it."

"So *you're* allowed to disrupt, but I'm not?"

"Do the math, Leo. I hurt you. One person. You might hurt three. Four, including yourself. More."

"How am I the enemy?"

She looks away again, blinking rapidly, thinking hard. It makes me happy she can't formulate an answer right away, but it's uncomfortable too. I say something to fill the silence. "It certainly seems nice, what you've created here. They seem great. I mean, Marcus switched the TV off after *Scooby-Doo* just like he was told to."

She smiles and her eyes go soft. "They're awesome."

"They're my sons," I say, not harshly. I just say it.

"Yes and no," she says.

"What?"

"They don't know you are, so you aren't."

"That's gibberish."

"Not to them."

"To you, you mean."

"We've got a good routine."

"That's the only downside, Marilyn? A different routine?"

She looks away again.

"Come on, just introduce me, as your friend at least. To start."

"They'd interrogate us," she says.

"I know!" I laugh, but she's not smiling.

"I'm not ready," she says, crossing her arms. "This is a shock."

"You must have imagined it would happen."

She thinks for a moment. "I thought it probably *should* happen, but I didn't think it would. I didn't want it to, and when you didn't come right after me, I thought you wouldn't ever come."

"Why did you leave?"

Again she looks away. I know she needs to in order to think, but I'm finding it irritating. A closed door. Now she looks down at the ground and taps one of her feet a few times. "You know what?" she says, finally looking at me, "I'm not doing this right now. I'm not having this conversation right now. We have plans."

"Oh. Sure. Well, I can find a hotel."

"A what? No!" she shouts, and then lowers her voice to a whisper. "Go home!"

"I don't —"

"Can we just . . . We need to do this properly. You should have written me a letter. Can you write me a letter?"

My face heats up. A *letter*? As if I've done something wrong? I almost refuse to promise to write. And then I remember I can promise anything, because I don't have to be honest. I can say anything I want to say. I can do what I want to do. So I say, "Sure I can," and smile at her very surprised face, and head back to my car.

I don't go straight home. I've found the boys, but that's all I've achieved, and it's not enough. I have to accept that Marcus would have breathed heavily through the gap at any unthreatening guy sitting on the top step. Leonardo would have thrown his two cents into the conversation with another guy too. I'm not their dad yet, to them. So I drive along their street until I can turn right, and then I turn right again, stopping one street away from them. I sit in my car, motor running, heat on, and I think. Then I find a diner and eat some breakfast. Once it's after ten, I park again on the street behind the boys' apartment and walk back around to their street. I pull up my hood and walk toward the building, watching the door in case they come out. Safely past the stairs, I lower my hood again and push the hardware store door open, jingling bells.

Christmas bulbs hang singly from the ceiling, a regular yard or so apart. Red, green, red, green, they hover above the shelves as if they wish they could fall. The effect isn't at all merry. Neither is the man who appears, looking more like a professor of hardware than a handyman. I was hoping for someone jovial. This might be difficult.

"Can I help you?" he asks, removing his reading glasses.

"I hope so," I say. "I've got a glass shelf in my kitchen, and it's sagging."

"Sagging?"

"Well, it's at an angle now. So weird. It's not a lot, but enough to make me feel like tiptoeing so the wine glasses don't suddenly slide off."

"I'd replace the whole thing," he says.

"Yeah, I'm sure that's the best idea, but it's a small kitchen, and my wife feels that glass shelves look less cluttered."

He thinks. "I can see that, yes."

"Fortunately we don't have boys upstairs like you do," I say, "otherwise I'm sure we'd have to do a total rethink."

He seems to chuckle. Not sure. It's subtle. "Let's look at brackets," he says. "This way."

I follow. When we stop in front of the right shelf, he says, "How long are your brackets? Do they extend the full width of the shelf?"

"Yes," I punt.

"Huh. So it's the wall, then. The glass isn't 'sagging', the wall is."

"Woah."

"Probably should get that checked out. In the meantime —"

An almighty thump from upstairs. Finally. The Christmas bulbs swing very slightly.

"Those two are quite a handful," I say.

He smiles. "Not too bad, most of the time."

"At least you won't be in here when they're jumping around with their Christmas presents," I say.

"They go to family anyway," he says.

And I have the information I need.

I reach out for a bracket, turn it in my hands. "So I don't need to change brackets, you think?" I'm amazed I can keep talking, my head feels so light.

"No," he says. "I'd say take the shelf down, and use a spirit level to – you have a spirit level? Yeah? Okay, use your spirit level to find out how much cardboard or whatever you need to put between the bracket and the wall – probably just the bottom of the bracket – to get the whole thing back to ninety degrees."

I thank him warmly and leave the store. I turn right, pull up my hood, and think about the best way to put things straight.

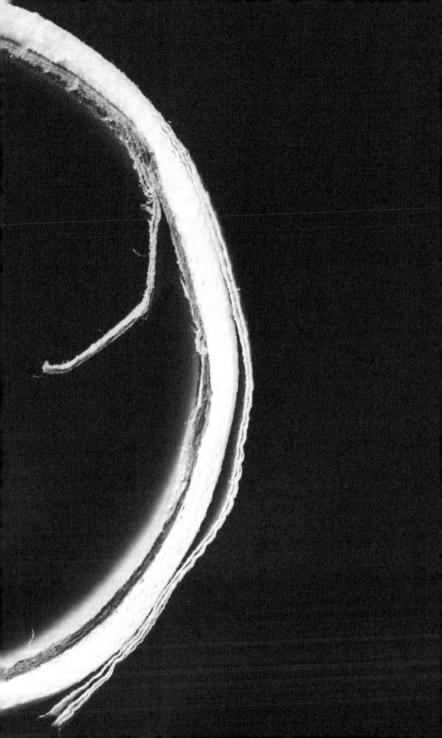

TWENTY-ONE

When I get home in the early afternoon, Liv is on the phone, looking worried. She was clearly interrupted making cookies. The counter is dusted with flour and cocoa and she has lined two baking trays with paper. I go to her and kiss her forehead and ask who she's talking to with my eyes. She mouths "Noriko".

While I get out of my coat she is saying, "I thought it was probably racoons when it happened here. . . Just one time, yeah. . . No, it was on. . . Okay, I'm going to tell Leo. It's probably fine. Your parents are probably right. But tell us if anything else weird happens. . . Yes. . . Of course. . . Okay. Leo's home now. I'll call you tomorrow. . . Okay. Bye."

"What happened to Noriko?"

"I can't say that anything really happened to her, but her outside trash can was on its side this morning like ours was the other day."

"Ours was on its side?"

"Yes, two days ago, I think."

"Why didn't you tell me?"

"Would you have told me?"

Liv goes to the fridge and takes out a log of chocolate-brown dough in plastic wrap while I think about this.

"No, you're right, I don't think I would have."

"Did you see the boys?"

"But the lid was still on?"

"Yes. I thought that was strange." She unwraps the dough.

"And the same thing happened at Noriko's?"

"Yes. And she got an envelope addressed to her with nothing inside it."

"Woah."

"I know, but her parents say it could have been one of their friends with early-onset Alzheimer's."

"What was the postmark?"

"Bridgewater."

"*Woah.*"

"But this friend of theirs lives in Bridgewater. They're going to visit her and see if they can figure out what she intended to send to Noriko. Never mind that for now! Did you see the boys?"

There's something I have to do before I can concentrate on telling her about the day. I hold up one finger. "I'll be right back," I say, and go out the back door again and over to where our big plastic trash can lives, next to the garage. The lid fits, but not very tightly, so we keep a big rock on top to deter racoons. I don't imagine that racoons can push over a big trash can like that from ground level, only by unbalancing it when they're on the lid, so I tilt it toward me and jump out of the way as the rock slides off and the can hits the ground. The lid pops off. I right it, and start to go back inside, but tell myself that once doesn't constitute a pattern. I pull it over three more times, and the lid pops off twice. If racoons pull our trash can over, there's only a twenty-five percent chance that the top will stay. But if someone creeps around the back of our house and carefully lays the trash can on its side, there is a one hundred percent chance of the lid staying on. What were the chances that the trash can lid at Noriko's would stay on if it was pulled over? Did they have a better lid, or a person – the same person? – creeping around?

"Well?" Liv asks, wiping down the counter, having understood what I went outside to do.

"The lid comes off most of the time when it is pulled over."

"But sometimes not?"

I don't give her the ratio. "Sometimes not."

"Probably nothing to worry about, then."

"That's right," I say, and hug her.

She feels me shiver and says, "You should have worn your coat."

"Give me a hot potato," I say, and she puts her mouth against my chest and blows wonderfully hot air through my shirts and onto my skin. Then she tips her head back.

"Okay, *now*. How did it go in Connecticut?"

I smile down at her, keeping her in my arms, and start telling her about the experience. After a few minutes, the timer goes and she leaves the embrace to take the cookies out of the oven. I continue talking, telling her how I want to go back, soon, the following weekend even, because I know they won't be there on Christmas.

"There are lawyers for this sort of situation, Leo," she tells me.

"I don't seem to care for eight years, and now I want rights? They'd have a field day with that."

"You have rights. Fathers have rights."

"Also, think about it. We don't have a lot of money, and Marilyn clearly has less. Can you imagine me using our savings and clearing out Marilyn's bank account too? That would be a terrible way to start a relationship with the boys."

"You're right. I can't imagine you doing that."

"That's why I want to go back over as Santa."

I'm completely serious, but Liv giggles.

"I'm not joking."

"How's that going to work?"

This 'going to' is encouraging. "Well, who would turn Santa away? Imagine: I go at about the same time as I did today, and when I knock, the face the boys see in the window is Santa. They'd let Santa in, right?"

Liv stops sliding the cookies onto a cooling rack and turns to me. "Leo," she says. "You *don't* want the boys opening the door to a stranger."

"Santa's not a stranger!"

"Yes, Leo, Santa is a stranger."

I put my hands in my pockets.

"What you're saying," she continues, "is that you want to do what Kjell did."

"No! Not really. I —"

"Where's the difference?"

"I wouldn't be planning to steal them."

"Trust me, Leo. Marilyn won't see it that way."

I don't know what to say to this. I'm so disappointed. I really enjoyed coming up with this plan on the way home, imagining lighting up the boys' faces, pushing aside the fact that seeing me again would darken Marilyn's, ignoring the fact that everything that happened after I got inside the apartment would be beyond my control.

"I was about to take a page out of Kjell's book, wasn't I?" I say.

She nods sadly.

"Can you forgive me for that?"

"Of course I can."

"Why?"

"He's a virus in your system now. It will take a while to recover from it."

I breathe in deeply through my nose and exhale. "Okay. Okay. So . . . I better think about composing that letter to Marilyn."

I try. I think about it driving to the college, between classes, and driving home, but I find it impossible to settle on the tone. Had I been serious about writing it when I promised I'd do it, I might have asked Marilyn about what she expected to be in it. I swing from a formal "Marilyn, As promised, I am writing you this letter to pave the way toward taking on more of a role in the boys' lives" to a cheerful "Hey Marilyn, I'm really looking forward to being available to you and the boys," trying out lots of first sentences in between but never getting any farther along. I think this is because none of these efforts feels like me. What *would* feel like me? Something pleasant and respectful would feel like the old me. Waiting for her answer, even if I didn't fully trust there would be one, would be the old me. I'm angry, though, and it gets harder and harder to focus on writing a letter that will open the door for me. The next weekend passes and I spend it imagining the boys watching cartoons and playing with Lego on their own when they don't have to be. More and more, I think about how Kjell made an audacious play for what he wanted.

Can I truly blame him, when for all he knew Liv had remained happy to see him even after he'd told her they were half-siblings? And the boys had been happy to see me, hadn't they? This feels like perfectly satisfactory logic, enough for me to tell Liv I'll be doing some secret Christmas shopping on the coming weekend, when in fact I'll be driving back to Connecticut.

I'm convinced I'm not pulling a *total* Kjell. It's not page from his book, just a few lines, because I *won't* go when the boys will be alone, and Marilyn will know who she's letting in the door. Even if the boys believe I'm Santa at first, I'll reveal myself pretty quickly, and maybe they'll remember me from two weeks before. She doesn't have to tell them I'm their father. They can think I'm just an old boyfriend. That won't be a lie. I decide to say that, in fact. When I pull down the beard to show them who I am, I'll say, "Remember me? Your mom's old friend?" And I'll say to Marilyn, "I'm just here as an old friend." If one of the boys says, "But she broke your heart!" I'll tell them, all of them, that it has healed very nicely. The boys might want to know my name. I think for a split second that I should tell them my middle name rather than my first name, in case Marilyn has told Leonardo that he was named after his father, but he'd be just Leo if she'd done that. I decide to let Marilyn decide what to call me. Maybe she'll jump in with a name, which I'll go along with. Or she'll warn me with her eyes and I'll come up with something. But I won't plan to lie. Not like Kjell. I want in, but once I'm in, I'll let Marilyn call the shots. I'll be physically there rather than applying to visit by letter, and Marilyn will have to deal with me, but I won't move in. I may be a crusader, but I will not be an occupying army.

I leave the college as early as I can on Tuesday to go over

to the mall in Brockton, in search of Lego for LeoNARdo, and something for Marcus. In the end I get Lego for Marcus, too. He did say he liked it. So now he'll have his own set and won't have to share. I can't find a Santa suit, though. I'm told to try a shop a half-hour away. I go home, and make an excuse to go upstairs for a bit, letting Liv think I'm hiding presents for her. I call directory assistance for the store's number. I dial the number I'm given, but it's early evening and they're closed. I can leave a message, though, and I beg them to call me back if they still have a Santa costume available. "Please please *please!*" I say in a way I hope they'll find funny.

I put the two boxes of Lego on the bed, and for a while I just stare at them.

I'm able to pick up a Santa suit, albeit one that is much too big for me, after work on Friday. The next morning I get up before Liv is awake. Once I'm dressed I sit by her on the bed and kiss her. She puts her arms around my waist and pulls her head up onto my thigh, asking me what time it is.

"Eight-thirty-ish," I tell her.

"You're leaving already?"

"It's a bit of a trek."

She rubs an eye. "You don't have to go to so much trouble, Leo. I'd be perfectly happy with a card."

"You know how it is when you get an idea you can't shake, though, right?"

She nods, and squeezes me. I stroke her hair. "Get some more sleep," I tell her, and go.

. . .

Once in Hamden I drive to the diner I ate in before. The coffee is still terrible, and it further fuels my excitement. Halfway through my eggs I urgently need the toilet. I take the Santa suit with me to the men's.

I don't put the belly-pillow in for the drive to the house, and the belt is too big without it, so that goes on the back seat too. Without the belly, the belt, the hat and the beard, I just feel like I've put pajamas on over my clothes. Scratchy, dangerous, 1970's polyester pajamas. Once I'm parked one street over, though, once I get the whole costume on and I'm holding the presents I wrapped in the funniest paper I could find, I feel better. I feel more worthy of attention, and ready to get it. Walking around the block I'm nervous, but it's mostly good-nervous. I have a memory of walking to a birthday party, a small boy holding a big gift. I remember a Halloween as the Michelin Man, scratched by the newspaper my mother stuffed into my suit of white garbage bags. I remember the *Will they like me?* feeling, but also the party feeling.

I'm not a snake in the grass. I'm bringing a party to the boys, as I imagine dads do.

Once I see the stairs, I'm worried that the sunny weather will mean Marilyn has taken the boys out to play somewhere, despite the cold. Maybe I've waited too long and missed the window of opportunity. I climb. There's frost partway up the glass of the door, and I can only see the empty hallway, not the floor where the boys were last time. I hear cutlery clinking on china, and a tap is turned on. Someone is washing dishes.

I knock.

"I'll get it," a child's voice announces. Rather than stepping aside and down onto the steps like I did last time, I stand back against the landing railing. This way the boy will have to open the door wide to see who I am. And he does. It's Marcus, the cartoon-lover. "Mom!" he shouts in awe. "It's Santa!"

"Oh?" I hear Marilyn say.

"Hi Marcus," I say.

"Hi," he says, and then Marilyn is next to him.

"Ho ho ho!" I say, hoping she'll recognize my voice. Before she can speak I say, "I've got something for Marcus and Leonardo. If I can just come in and put them down. I won't stay long."

Right on cue, Marcus says, "Sure!" and gets out of the way. Marilyn obviously wants to bar the door, but she can't make herself do it. I hold out the two presents and step forward and Marilyn moves out of my way, reflexively polite, just as I was when Kjell arrived at my door. Marcus tries to see if the gifts have anything on them identifying who they're for, and I'm saying, "Shall I put these on the couch?" when a door off the hallway opens and Leonardo comes running out, laughing. I didn't see him laugh last time. He was so serious.

And then Kjell follows.

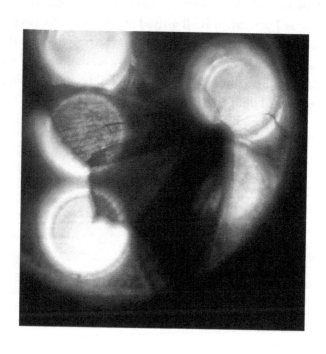

TWENTY-TWO

I'm aware of Leonardo skidding to a stop when he sees Santa, but I'm looking at Kjell. I watch him register a man in a Santa costume — his eyes express something like *I wonder who this friend is.* Can he perceive Marilyn's discomfort from behind? Is he close enough to see the horror in my eyes? Marcus goes to his brother and pulls him toward me from the hallway and says, "Look, two presents!"

I feel foolish. The emotion is so powerful that I wish I could disappear, rewind, never have met Marilyn, never have met Liv even. But the boys' hands are on the presents I'm still holding, and they're trying to turn them over, and the part of my brain that can still function analytically realizes I've got their attention and I can keep it. I dig deep down inside myself for a warm and jovial voice. "Now these are for Christmas, boys," I say. "Let's sit over here on the couch, and you can tell me where you're going for Christmas, and what you're hoping for." There's no way I'm taking the beard off now. I move to the couch and sit. My heart pounds and blood swishes in my ears. Marcus clambers onto my lap. I shift Marcus onto one leg so I can invite Leonardo onto the other.

"We're going to Nana's," Marcus says.

"Andy Poppy's," Leonardo says, climbing up. "Nana's and Poppy's."

In my peripheral vision I see Kjell step farther into the room, but I ignore him.

"Uh-huh? And what are you going to eat?"

"*Leo*," Marilyn says sharply. Leonardo and I both look up at her.

"Leo?" says Kjell and leans forward to scrutinize my eyes. Then he begins to laugh. The only word to describe the sound is 'triumphant'.

Oh, my God. He's been *waiting* for me.

His laugh steals some of Marilyn's thunder. She says, "Please stop this," less sharply.

"What?" asks Leonardo.

"Not you, honey," Marilyn says.

"Why?" I ask her.

"Don't stop," interjects Kjell, surprising Marilyn. "This is fantastic." He crouches to sit on the rug and leans back on his palms. "Carry on!"

I find I have to clear my throat before I can talk again. While I do, Leonardo says, "Your name's Leo?"

I should look at Marilyn, follow her lead like I planned to, but it's not Marilyn I'm up against anymore. "It is," I tell him. "The real Santa only comes on Christmas." Then I jut my chin at Kjell and ask Leonardo, "What's that man's name?"

Marcus pipes up. "That's Morten."

I stare at Kjell, and the bastard winks at me.

I turn my head slowly to look at Marilyn, instinctively

tightening my grip on the boys. "That is not his name," I tell her.

Marcus says quietly in my ear, "I only eat stuffing and cranberry sauce."

I turn my face to him and whisper, "Yum!" I show him a big smile, or I try to, but the moustache and beard are so luxurious I doubt he can see it. Inside, I'm suddenly feeling sad. Having the boys on my lap feels so natural that I spin into grief for the lost years.

Marilyn breaks the silence. "Boys," she says, "what do you say we let you open these presents before Christmas?"

"Yay!" they both shout. I give them each the one I intended for them and they start tearing at the paper.

"Hang out over there and play while the grown-ups do some talking," she tells them, and I slide them off my lap as they're exclaiming over what they've received. I want to watch them play – I want to play *with* them – but both Kjell and I do as we're told, standing up to join Marilyn in the kitchen area.

Just looking at Kjell again drags me back up out of sadness and into the clarity of fury. "Here's what we're going to do," I say, taking control before Marilyn can tell me off. "If you don't want me to tell the boys who I really am, then I won't tell you who Morten really is. I recommend finding out, though. For your safety."

Marilyn looks at Kjell, who has a bewildered face on. "Morten?"

Kjell shakes his head with an innocent show of palms. "I don't know this man."

Marilyn looks at him still. He shakes his head again.

Turning back to me she asks, "Is this some sort of blackmail?"

"No. Not at all. I assure you, you will thank me."

I glance at Kjell and I see him calculating. He looks like he wants to say something, so I start calculating as well. If he's about to admit who he really is, thinking Marilyn might give him a break for being honest with her, I can't bank on her letting me tell the boys who I am, ever. He takes a breath in and I announce, "It's okay! It's okay, it's okay. I've done what I came to do. This has been great. He is *not* named Morten. And this has been great."

I stride to the door, open it and step out into the cold. I give the boys a little wave before I close the door, and head down to the sidewalk. I start to walk away slowly, my breath shallow and fast, my mouth so dry I need to get to water soon. I try for what I hope looks like a contented saunter, and before long I hear what I've been waiting for, the bang of Marilyn's door, the thud of her feet as she runs down the steps. She's decided to trust me, and wants to get the truth, so I'm smiling when I turn around, but it's Kjell bearing down on me and I have no time to dodge him before shoves me backwards toward the street. Above his head I can see that Marilyn has come out and is watching from the landing.

"Nice admission of guilt, Kjell," I shout, so she can hear his name, and he shoves me harder this time, sending me backwards off the curb. I land on my back and knock my head and he's on me, pinning me, not caring to look right or left for cars. Pin me is all he does, though. In a flash I realize that's all he *can* do. Even enraged he's smart enough to know that maiming or killing me won't get him where he wants to be – which is where we were five minutes ago, with me writhing on a pin like a moth and him feeling like he'd won. There's no way back there.

It's very hard to breathe, but I'm not scared now. I push

my voice hoarsely through the crooked beard: "Now what, Kjell?"

He just pants.

"Is this part of your clever plan too?"

After a second he sits back, stressing my bladder, the pillow between us making him look even taller than he is. He inhales deeply. "No. You know, this isn't so much fun anymore."

"*Fun?*" Marilyn says from behind him, startling us both, and then a car goes by, screeches to a halt, and backs quickly up. I hear an automatic window go down and a voice say, "The fuck? You okay, Santa?"

When I tip my head back to try and see the person, my hat stays put and my eyes end up behind the fake fur, which suddenly makes me want to giggle. "I'm okay," I say.

"Is this a medical situation?" the voice says.

Now I do laugh, and I take advantage of having a witness. "No, it's okay. We've sorted it out. You can get up now, Kjell." Kjell gets to his feet and extends a hand to help me up as well, raising the other hand in a wave to the driver. I don't take his hand, but I do get to my feet. I adjust my hat, and my beard. It might make sense to take it off, but I've become attached to it.

"Okay, then," the driver says, and moves on. Marilyn is standing on the sidewalk with her hands on her hips, looking at Kjell in shock, and something else too. She looks like a mother – a disgusted, disappointed mother. I start to feel giddy. I giggle. Poor little baby Kjell and his need to screw around in everyone's business to get attention. I start to really laugh. I double over, and when I come back up and look at Kjell again it makes me laugh more. Poor little baby Kjell who wants love so much and stomps on it when he gets it. I hoot and it's a massive release of energy. I'm so happy. I've never been this kind of happy. The feeling bubbles in my chest and my feet just have to move, so I skip out into the empty street and break into a run with my arms out like airplane wings. When I swing back around, they're both watching me. I've decided never to talk to him again. I stop by Marilyn, pulling off my hat and facial hair. We watch Kjell and he watches us.

"What did he tell you he did for a living?" I ask Marilyn.

"He's a math teacher," she replies.

"Uh-huh? At our house he was a soccer coach."

Kjell seems to smirk at his creativity.

"What has he got against you, Leo?" Marilyn asks.

"A loose screw. A totally screwed up loose screw. How about we go inside?"

"Let me explain," Kjell says, but Marilyn takes me firmly by the arm and pulls me close to her.

"Let's go back inside," she says, and we walk around him and toward her stairs. It takes everything I have not to look back over my shoulder. I listen for footsteps, almost sure that Kjell will take another run at me, but they don't come. Instead, he shouts.

"You'll never get rid of me, Leo!"

I don't reply. Marilyn's grip on my arm is almost painful now.

"I'll leave, but I'll never be *gone*," he continues. "You'll always know that I *fucked* your wife, and I *fucked* your best friend, and I *fucked* the mother of your children!"

We're halfway up the stairs now. I let myself look over at him and he's beginning to look a bit smaller. My legs feel like Jell-o, but under my breath I say, "Whatever."

Once we're at the top I tell Marilyn I'll stay outside until I see him go.

"Okay," Marilyn says, and starts to open the door but then she closes it again and stands beside me. "Safety in numbers," she says, and we fold our arms like bouncers. Kjell has his hands on his hips now, and he's staring at the sidewalk, shaking his head as if he can't believe what a silly mix-up there's been. He looks up at us with a smile that's supposed to look like he knows he's just too smart to be understood, and he's truly sorry that we're not able to keep up. For once I don't worry about choosing an expression. I just leave my face flat, nothing on it for him to read. For a moment he looks like he will say something, but then he shakes his head again, and turns, and jogs away to his car.

When we can't hear his engine anymore I say, "Change your lock if you gave him a key."

"I didn't, but I think I'll move," she says.

"Don't put in a forwarding order."

"Good idea."

"But, um, let me know where you go?"

"I will," she says. "Come inside."

She holds the door for me and I go back in where it's warm, and climb out of the Santa suit. I sit on the rug with the boys.

I play.

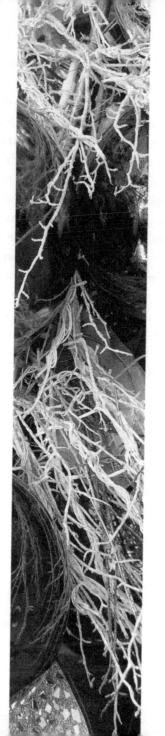

TWENTY-THREE

It's Christmas Eve: electric candles in the window, little white lights on the tree, pork-belly ribs in the oven. We're doing the big dinner today, the Norwegian way, rather than on the 25th, and we've got Noriko and Alice coming. I shoot a few photographs straight down into our trash can. Layers of see-through plastic; layers of Christmas. I fool around with which images on which packaging to focus on until Liv tells me to get peeling or the potatoes won't be ready on time.

The kitchen smells wonderful. So does the living room. Liv dried orange slices and hung them in a sort of wreath from the big central lamp. I don't feel like we're in Massachusetts. I know Liv doesn't want to go to Norway for a while, maybe a long while, but I think I'd like to. I'd like to see Karin again, now that the air has cleared. I'd like to see her and Liv together again. Maybe next Christmas we can go over. Actually, maybe the boys will be with us next Christmas, or we'll be with them. Maybe Marilyn will agree to share them for some of the day. She *has* agreed for me to take them out for one Saturday every six weeks. As Leo, not yet as Dad. I didn't fight about that. I'm taking the long view.

As always, we flinch and expect the worst when someone comes to the door, but tonight it's only our invited guests knocking. Nothing strange has occurred since I last saw Kjell, in Hamden. Maybe he's trying to ruin other lives now. Or maybe he has merely settled down to wait another fourteen years before trying to ruin ours again. He's out there some-where in the world, and that's oppressive, but I know not to open the door to him now. I know to laugh at him. I wish I'd known that all along.

White tablecloth, four unlit red candles. I'm seated opposite Alice, who is dressed in black velvet and yellowed lace. Noriko, in a fluffy red sweater, is seated opposite Liv's chair. Liv is bringing the food to the table. The platter of pork has sprigs of holly around the edge. Liv lights the candles, takes off her apron, and turns out the light, and Alice, Noriko and I make appreciative noises. I can see Liv's smile in the candle-light. She is looking down, getting her napkin onto her lap, but her smile can't be hidden that way. She picks up her glass of spiced wine before looking at our faces.

"Thank you for coming," she says to the women. "I'm so glad you're here."

Noriko says, "I'm so glad you're back, honey," and Alice says, "I'm so glad I'm not *dead*."

We drink, and I pick up the carving knife and start cutting portions of pork. "This okay for you, Alice?" I ask, and she says, "For a start, sure," and lifts her plate.

I cut into the meat again and I'm about to ask Noriko the same question when I hear Liv say, "You okay, Nori?"

I look at Noriko, and she's staring wide-eyed at Liv, and then she clears her throat, and swallows, and says, "Excuse me for a second." She gets up quickly and hurries out of the room. I look at Liv, and can hear that Noriko hasn't just gone into the living room. She's hauling up the stairs.

"I'll go," Liv says, and follows her.

"Don't mind if I start?" Alice asks me.

"No, please eat while it's hot," I say, and serve myself some pork before inviting Alice to try the potatoes and pickled cabbage.

"Delicious," she says. "Oh my, yes."

I take a bite and listen to my teeth crunch through the skin.

"What do you think's going on?" she says more quietly.

"I don't know," I say. "Noriko doesn't get sick much."

"Huh," Alice says, and drinks. "This drink, so many spices it," she says.

"Yeah."

"And pickled things. All these traditional foods, it's about preserving, and jazzing old stuff up, and getting nutrition in hard times." She puts another bite in her mouth and talks as she chews. "I find it, I don't know, poignant."

"The good old days were hard times, you mean?"

"Come on," she says. "All days are hard times."

I look at her face and her eyes are twinkling, but it must just be the candles because her mouth is somber.

"You're a photographer?" she says. I'm grateful for how she presses on with conversation because all I can think about is what's going on upstairs.

"Uh-huh."

"How long since someone last took my picture, I wonder. Oh, jeez, it's gotta be twenty-some-odd years."

"I'll take your picture," I tell her.

"Nah. I need too much jazzing up."

"No, I mean it. Stay right there."

I go to the basement and get my camera. Back at the table, I move all four candles closer to her.

"My hair is dumb," she says.

"Don't worry. It's not well lit."

She wipes her mouth with her napkin.

"Turn toward the back door, okay? I want to try a profile. The shape of the lace is interesting from the side."

There's only time for a couple of shots. I'd love to get an image with focus on both the texture of the lace and the extremely varied topography of Alice's face, somehow, but Liv comes back in the kitchen and sits.

"She's lying down," she tells us.

I put down my camera and move the candles back to their original positions. "She doesn't think she can eat at all?"

Liv puts her napkin back on her lap, shaking her head. "Too nauseous."

"What a shame. You want some?"

"Um, yes please."

I cut Liv some pork, and Alice moves the side dishes over to her. Liv thanks her, and asks, "How are you, Alice?"

"I'm perfect," Alice says. "Food, wine. Perfect. What happened to your friend, that's the question."

Liv throws me a look I don't get. "Well," she starts, "she's . . ." She doesn't seem to know what to say.

"She's a nurse," I interrupt. "Doesn't she know what's wrong with her?"

"She suspects," Liv says.

"Uh-oh," says Alice.

Liv cuts her meat.

"What?" I say.

"'*Suspects*'," Alice says, as if her emphasis on the word will make things clear to me.

"What?" I say again.

A message seems to pass between Alice and Liv. Alice shrugs and pushes food onto her fork with her knife. "It's a feeling like no other," she says, holding the fork in front of her mouth. "Unless she's been seasick."

I understand now.

I listen to Alice's teeth crunch through the skin.

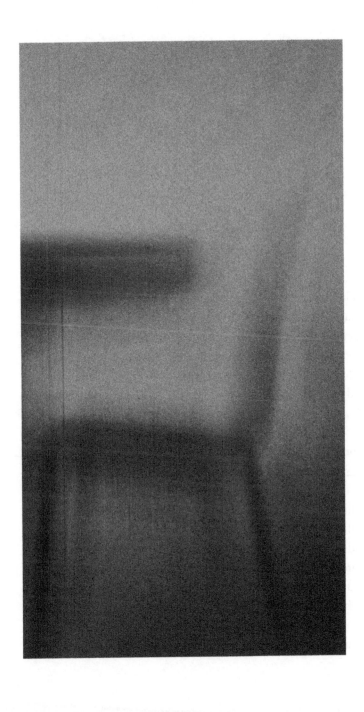

ACKNOWLEDGMENTS

The first moment of this book came to me in a half-dreaming state between sleeping and waking in 1995. None of the people involved were Norwegian in that initial vision, but I'd recently been the *forlover* (maid of honor) at the wedding in Norway of my best friend from college, and was still very taken with the experience. Thank you, Eva Robbins and Jim Garrity.

I wrote the first draft in 1995 and 1996. I had a baby, though, and life got busier, and I let things pile up on the novel. I picked it up again in 2000, did some work on it, and sent it to an agent in New York who loved the first three chapters and asked to see the rest . . . which he didn't like at all. I put it down again. I wrote a new draft in 2006, I think. I added a new character and took him out again some years later. All along the way, people read it and encouraged me, but it has been so long in development that I can't remember who they all are. If you are one of the unnamed, thank you!

I'm grateful to my late father, Jim Lester, one of the first enthusiastic readers, without whose very old emails about it I would have lost the document. I'm also grateful to my brother, Toby Lester, and my friends Robert Stern, Aileen Chen, Victoria Peattie Helm, and Nick and Catherine Phillips for their insights, fact-checks, proofreading, and cheerleading. I am indebted to Susan Davis of Jericho Writers for her in-depth manuscript review and recommendations. For help with understanding memory and cognitive rehabilitation techniques, I consulted Dr. Elizabeth Glisky, Professor Emerita of psychology at Arizona State University — both at the first-draft stage and two decades later. Without Ann Keating, I wouldn't have understood how one went looking for someone in the pre-Internet days. For the beauty of this product, and the deep sense of joy in the process of publishing it, I cannot thank Andy, my husband, my helpmeet, enough.

ABOUT THE ARTIST

Andrew Gurnett is a photographic artist based in Worcestershire, England. Previously, he spent over 20 years living in Singapore. His work has featured in group and solo exhibitions, in photographic books, and on the walls of private collectors and of a 5-star hotel. He loves the unintentional beauty of the everyday and the stories that are told by the functional, forgotten and discarded.

www.andrewgurnett.com

 facebook.com/andrew.gurnett.photo.art

twitter.com/AndrewGurnett

 instagram.com/gurnettphotoart

ABOUT THE AUTHOR

Alison Jean Lester spent many of her formative years in Massachusetts before studying, working and writing in Indiana, China, Washington DC, Italy, Taiwan, Japan and Singapore. She is the author of the novels *Lillian on Life* and *Yuki Means Happiness*, the collections *Locked Out: Stories Far from Home* and *Restroom Reflections: How Communication Changes Everything*, and the memoir *Absolutely Delicious: A Chronicle of Extraordinary Dying*, a finalist in the Indie Excellence Books Awards. Daughter of a mother from the Wirral Peninsula and a father from Missouri, she now lives with her husband in Worcestershire, England.

www.alisonjeanlester.com

facebook.com/alisonjeanlester

twitter.com/A_J_Lester

PRAISE FOR ALISON JEAN LESTER

Like the waitress who pulls the bottom of her kimono "into the perfect position" for kneeling by Diana's table in a restaurant, Lester has constructed her novel like an elegant piece of origami, every element deftly arranged into something as close to perfection as I can imagine.

LUCY SCHOLES FOR *THE NATIONAL* ON
YUKI MEANS HAPPINESS

Dazzling . . . Spiked with unflinching observations, riotous riffs and poignant reflections.

THE WASHINGTON POST ON *LILLIAN ON LIFE*

Absolutely Delicious is like a gift. It is tender, light-footed, funny, painful and gallant, and in writing with courage and wit about dying well, Lester has written about living well.

NICCI GERRARD, NOVELIST AND AUTHOR
OF *WHAT DEMENTIA TEACHES US ABOUT LOVE* ON *ABSOLUTELY DELICIOUS: A CHRONICLE OF EXTRAORDINARY DYING*